# Sword and Sorcery

# Also by John Ricks

**Freddy Anderson Chronicles:**

*Freddy Anderson's Home*
(Book One in the Freddy Anderson Chronicles)

*Protectress*
(Book Two in the Freddy Anderson Chronicles)

# Sword and Sorcery

## Short Stories Book 1

## John Ricks

iUniverse, Inc.
Bloomington

## Sword and Sorcery
## Short Stories Book 1

iUniverse books may be ordered through booksellers or by contacting:

iUniverse
1663 Liberty Drive
Bloomington, IN 47403
www.iuniverse.com
1-800-Authors (1-800-288-4677)

ISBN: 978-1-4759-3969-9 (sc)
ISBN: 978-1-4759-3970-5 (hc)
ISBN: 978-1-4759-3971-2 (e)

Library of Congress Control Number: 2012913106

Printed in the United States of America

iUniverse rev. date: 09/13/2012

This book is dedicated to potato chips. Crunchy, yum.

# Contents

# Table of Gods

1. Sobel      (God of War/Sun)
2. Ultio      (God of Retribution)
3. Advorsa      (God of Slaughter)
4. Brevis      (God of Gnomes)
5. Callosus      (God of Evil Giants and Orcs)
6. Commeatus      (God of Travel)
7. Dimidims      (Goddess of Halflings)
8. Drajuris      (God of Good Dragons)
9. Draquae      (Goddess of Evil Dragons)
10. Magicum      (God of Magic)
11. Malificus      (God of Tyranny and Hells)
12. Malum      (God of Secrets)
13. Mortisma      (Goddess of Death Magic)
14. Natura      (Goddess of Nature)
15. Oprepo      (Goddess of Rogues)
16. Pola      (Goddess of Dwarves)
17. Potentis      (God of Strength/Good Giants)
18. Pravus      (God of Death)
19. Proba      (God of Elves)
20. Sanus      (Goddess of Music)
21. Silvestris      (God of Nature)
22. Valoris      (God of Valor)

# Currency Standard

1. Paper money (worthless)
2. Copper
3. Silver (one silver is ten copper)
4. Gold (one gold is ten silver)
5. Platinum (one platinum is ten gold)
6. Small gold bar (one bar is one hundred gold or ten platinum)
7. Small platinum bar (one bar is one hundred platinum or ten gold bars)

The value of gems is dependent on weight (measured in carats) and clarity. The prices listed are for one carat of fair clarity. Poor clarity is half the price; a perfect stone ten times the price. The value of diamonds is also dependent on depth of color. For a clear diamond, the less color, the higher the price. For a colored diamond, the more color, the higher the price. A red diamond that has a light red or pink color is worth much less than a deep red (blood) diamond that is difficult to see through.

8. Garnet (10 gold) very common
9. Sapphire (100 gold) common
10. Ruby (100 platinum) scarce
11. Emerald (200 platinum) very scarce
12. Clear diamond (500 platinum) rare
13. Black diamond (1,000 platinum) very rare
14. Blue diamond (10,000 platinum) exceptionally rare
15. Blood diamond (25,000 platinum) extraordinarily rare

# Introduction

*Sword and Sorcery* is about fighters, wizards, rogues, clerics, adventuring parties, and adventure. It was written to help readers picture in their minds the type of adventurer one might have met in a time when dragons were flying overhead and every turn could provide a deadly surprise. Each type of adventurer is at a specific point in his life, some just beginning and some very powerful. This book was written for children everywhere, be they age ten or one hundred.

# The Bard

I walked into the tavern, stomped the snow and ice off my feet, and looked all around without letting on that I was surveying the place, without moving my head, without giving away that I was looking. It was still early, so there were few customers. I glanced at myself in the mirror and saw a clean-cut man in his thirties with long blond hair and a perfect nose. The disguise was still working. I pulled the cloak a little tighter. The ones I was hunting were not here. At the bar was an old man drinking away his sorrows. There were two merchants haggling in the center of the room at a long table made for six chairs. Both wore swords and dirks, and one actually looked like his were usable. The other's were overly ornate, over polished, and over oiled. There was a fat black cat by the low fire with three white boots and a white streak on its face above the nose and between the eyes. It was watching a mouse picking out crumbs on the wooden floor about fifteen feet across the room to the side, where the floor had been swept into a pile of dirt and crumbs.

The bartender was watching me. A very pretty, but far too young, serving wench was waiting to see what I would do. Smells from the kitchen were good, and I was hungry. I crossed to the fireside and took a chair at a small table for one, with my back to the corner and my face to the rest of the room, where I could watch the stairs. The serving wench came over, swaying in a provocative way and showing a little too much leg.

As she bent over the table to wipe it off with a dirty rag, her tiny bosoms nearly fell out of the top of a very loose dress. She asked, "Is there something I can get for you, my lord?"

I had not taken off my cloak and the hood was still up. She could not see any part of me. I said, "Yes. I am in need of a room for a few nights, a bath, and food."

"I'll send Mac over and he can take care of the room and bath. Lunch is being served. Stew from last night with fresh baked bread. What would you like to drink?"

"Water. Lemon or lime juice if you have it."

"We have apple juice, cider, grog, or mulled wine. Beer and good wines are available."

Mulled wine sounded good right now. The warmed spiced beverage of this region would be welcome in my nearly frozen stomach. "I'll have water and a tankard of the mulled wine."

I did not bring out any money so her eyes narrowed and she said, "That will be two copper for the food and a copper for the mulled wine."

I remembered the last time I paid in advance. I received burnt meat surprise, three-day-old bread—and very little of that—and the wine was nearly undrinkable and came long after I ordered. I took a couple of silver pieces from my pouch and said, "I'll pay and tip when I receive and approve of the food and drink."

She smiled when she saw the silver and quickly turned and nearly ran off to the kitchen. She yelled at the bartender when she passed. "He has silver and needs a bath and bed, daddy."

The bartender slowly came around the corner of the bar and made his way toward my table. His walk, size, and the well-worn great spiked club hanging from his belt told me that this bar gets busy and he does the bouncing. He asked, "I hear you need a room and bath, sir?"

"Two or possibly three nights, and a hot bath today, after lunch."

"I have a single room for one silver a night, or you can share with the two merchants for three copper a night. The bath is two copper. Both are paid up front."

"The single is a closed room with a fresh bed?"

"It has a door and lockable shutters. I'll have the boy change out the hay in the bed for another copper."

"That will be fine. The bath is fresh water?"

"Three days sitting but not used yet."

"Iron or brass tub?"

"Iron."

I said, "Water in an iron tub smells like rust after a day or two. Change the water and I'll pay three copper for the bath."

"Done."

I paid him four silver and he returned six copper and then he asked, while thumbing his club, "You're not here to start any kind of trouble, are you?"

"Not that I am aware of."

"Three rules in this place. One, leave my daughters alone. Pinch or smack their bottoms hard enough to leave a mark and I'll return the favor. Two, fights inside will cost the winner cleanup fees. Blood is hard to scrub out of the floor. Three, let people have fun. They come here to drink and forget their lives and wives for a little while. Let them."

"I understand, but I will protect myself if someone becomes violent."

"You should. Try not to kill unless absolutely necessary. Tends to cut down on repeat customers."

He turned and went back to the bar. It wasn't long before the young wench came out with a full plate of fresh, hot stew with lots of meat in it and a full loaf of bread with plenty of butter. A younger sister was carrying the water and the mulled wine. They set them down, and I tried the stew. It was hot and good. The mulled wine was very good, and I paid for both and tipped both the girls well. The little one looked at the two coppers I gave her and had no idea what to do with them.

The older bent down and whispered, "Put it away like I showed you, and don't let Momma know." She tucked them into her dress top, and as she turned to leave, they dropped out the bottom. I coughed and they turned. I motioned toward the floor. The little one opened her dress and looked all over for her coins and then snatched the coins off the floor and ran for the kitchen.

The older girl whispered, "Thank you, my lord," and then turned to leave with a smile.

I sat there enjoying my lunch and watching everything that happened. My anger and pain I kept to myself. Eventually my bath was ready and the serving wench led me to a room in the back with a tub full of hot, fresh water and soap. I started to undress until I noticed she was watching, so I took her arm and gently led her out and closed the door. I put a chair against the door and jammed it shut. I checked the shutters and placed my dagger between the handles to ensure they remained closed. Then I took off my cloak, haversack, quiver, leather armor, boots, and weapons. I climbed into the water and it felt wonderful. It was my first hot bath in a month of traveling. I let the soapy water soak into my body and warm my sprit. I scrubbed every stitch of clothing I had and hung them up to dry, and I then relaxed in the water for two hours while thinking about my loss. It was hot and moist in the tub room, but the cold air from outside was creeping in and I needed to check out my bedroom. I reluctantly stood up and used the pail of water on the side to rinse. It was not hot, and I yelled when the snowmelt hit my skin. There was a knock on the door.

"Are you all right, my lord?"

"I am fine, but next time, HEAT THE RINSE WATER!"

There were giggles and a, "Yes, my lord."

I performed a song called "Undampen," which dried my clothing and me. I put away my traveling clothes and donned performing clothes. I put away most of my weapons and took my dagger down from the window and sheathed it in my boot. I kept eight throwing daggers hidden in my pants and shirt. Then I put my cloak on to cover up what I was wearing and to hide my face. I unblocked the door, picked up my haversack and quiver, and walked out.

The girls were right there waiting. This was a perfect time for them to take a bath without having to carry in and heat more water. Besides, their mother did not want to waste expensive soap for the bath or wood for the fire. They shut the door after them. I walked past the cook and said to their mother, "Very good lunch. Thank you." She smiled but said nothing.

I walked out to the main room and the bartender said, "Top of the stairs, first door on the right. Best room I have. The bed has already been changed, and I saw to it he did it right. Don't have a cleric or wizard around to do a spell to keep the bugs away."

I said, "They charge too much. Besides, I can do that myself."

His eyebrows rose just a little. "Y … yes, my lord. How long will the spells be good for?"

I knew what he was trying to find out. The longer the spell lasted, the more powerful the caster—and the lower he had better grovel. I hate the way people are made to bow down to others. I said, "Long enough." I climbed the stairs and took the first room to the right. It was a nice room, if somewhat simple, and smelled of fresh hay. The quilt was old and a little worn, but thick and cozy looking. There was a fireplace, and wood was stacked, but it was too early in the day to be lighting a fire for warmth. Firewood costs if you don't cut it yourself, and most tavern owners haven't the time. When this one's son and daughters are older perhaps things will change.

I put my haversack and quiver down and did a conjuration spell for my harp case and a good book. I took off my cloak and then returned to the main room and took that same seat by the fire.

The tavern owner saw my face and bowed. The perfect face, bold chin, small nose, and blond hair with blue eyes could only mean one thing: high class, possibly royalty—a baron's son or higher. The clothes said average wealth but not poor, and magic user—but not what kind. He saw the harp case and his eyes lit up. "You know how to play that harp, my lord?"

I said, "I am learning." The fact is, I have been trained by top bards in the royal court and am better than most. With my artifact harp of emotion, I am far better than any other. I placed the harp near my feet and opened the book. It was a good book—*Elostand the Wise*. According to the book, he was not as wise as he was very lucky. I continued to watch the comings and goings while taking time for dinner. As night fell, more people started showing up: men, women, children, and all their relatives. Everyone who came in took seats where they could look my direction. The children were seated up front, closer to me than the grownups. A harpist is a treat they don't get out here very often. Not at the end of known lands, the northern side of nowhere, the crossroads between no place and never been, the town called One Corner.

I marked the page with a piece of linen and closed the book while saying to myself, "Good book." I looked around and pretended surprise. I motioned for the young serving wench to come over, and she did, even though she was very busy bringing drinks to nearly thirty people. The room was overly crowded.

She asked, "Yes, my lord?"

"Two things. Water would be nice, and what are all these people doing staring at me?"

She smiled and yelled out, "Water!" across the room. One of the other girls raised her hand and yelled, "Got it!" Then she turned back to me and said, "They are waiting for you to play that harp." She turned with a smile and walked away.

I looked around the room and directly into some of the children's eyes and picked up the book. The disappointment was nearly palpable. One girl started to tear up, but she stopped when she saw me hold the book up and it disappeared. They clapped. This was going to be an easy crowd. Then *they* entered.

It was a party of five adventurers: a lawful good paladin of Solbelli, wielding a great sword slung over his shoulder and wearing plate armor all shiny and clean; a cleric of Solbelli in his plate armor with symbols of his deity in places to show off his love for his god; a thief they called a rogue from the capital city with a rapier and quiver moving silently through the crowd; a barbarian from the plains, full of muscle and looking ready to snap a person in two; and a dwarf fighter with twin axes who appeared to be amused by the people. They were a powerful-looking group, and people quickly got out of their way. I recognized them as the five that had broken into my home, killed my wife and two children, killed my guards, and taken my property. I had been following them for sixteen weeks. There they were, and I had ten children sitting expectantly in front of me. There was nothing I could do just yet. I needed to work the crowd.

I turned to a man that looked like he was in charge of something. Old and wise, strong and sure. "Good Sir, I am just a simple bard, passing through, who happens to also play a harp. I don't know how good or bad I will be, and I don't want to disappoint these people."

The man said, "I am the sheriff, and I can assure you, my lord, if you can play at all, we will be most pleased."

I smiled and reached for my harp case. I wanted to scream and reach for a weapon, but I needed to carry this out. I alone could not take them.

I placed the case on an empty table near me and opened it up.

The harp inside was one of exquisite beauty. Simple, yet elegantly carved of pure dragon ivory. It was one single piece, carved from a grand red dragon's tooth. The strings were platinum, and the red diamonds in the neck and soundboard were glowing in the firelight. I positioned the harp in my lap, and just before starting, I stopped and turned to the children. "Forgive me a second as I play a simple piece to warm up."

One of the boys said, "Sure."

A girl tapped him hard on the head and chastised him. "Where's your manners?"

He put a hand on his head, rubbing the spot, and said, "Sure, my lord."

I smiled and started playing a very basic piece—at least basic for advanced bards in the queen's court. The sudden and complete silence said it all. I played without emotion, but it was enough to bring joy and wonderment to the little crowd. The adventurers paid little attention but stayed quiet. They ordered dinner and ate in musical silence.

I looked at the boy when I was finished "warming up" and said, "Now I'm ready."

Cheers and clapping echoed off the walls, making them seem louder than they really were. I looked at the adventurers and sadness gripped me. I played a piece so old time could not remember, so new time would never forget, and so sad even the gods cried. I was in tears the entire time, and the tears absorbed into the harp as they dripped down my face. When I was finished, a girl came up to me crying and gave me a hug. The old and wise sheriff said, "Lost someone close to you recently, son?"

I said to them, "My entire family was murdered by a group of adventurers. I am sorry. It is difficult for me to play when I can so recently remember the joy my children had at listening to me. Let me try something happier. Something my boy would have liked."

He nodded. I turned the harp to me and played a tune that had people up and dancing, children clapping and laughing, the sheriff remembering good times, and the gods were smiling. Then I tried one the queen always enjoys this time of year. A peaceful song that speaks of warm fires, cozy beds, and a relaxing book. My voice was strong and quiet, and I was in great form. Each sound, each syllable, was perfect and something to cherish. Even the boy was hugging his sister.

I was ready. It had to be done. I could wait no longer. My next song spoke of dragons and demons and caused wonderment at the beauty of flight. The sheriff was smiling like he remembered the days when he had flown. Then I turned to a story of great sadness. I told them how five adventurers had entered my home and destroyed everyone I have ever loved. How they had done this only because I was not human and this gave them the right to kill my wife and children. They rose in anger when I said, "And they are eating dinner in this very tavern right now."

Outrage poured from the children and parents and they changed into their true demon forms. The five had no chance. It happened so fast they didn't have time to pull weapons. They died in the carnage of the very quick and one-sided battle. The sheriff himself ate the paladin. I stayed two more days, celebrating with the little demons and their parents and helping with magic where I could. Most of my time was spent telling great stories of some of the most powerful of our kind and the battles the humans had forced us into to protect our realms.

# The Druid

The little princess entered the breakfast chamber and found, to her pleasant surprise, that her father was there eating. She walked up to him and gave him a hug, which he returned gladly.

"It is nice to see you, daughter. You are very radiant today. Is this a special day? Did I forget a birthday or anniversary?"

The princess said, "No, Father, I have been happy a lot lately."

The king said, "I am not complaining, you understand, but what is causing you this great happiness? It is not your norm."

She said, "Every day, for weeks now, a little songbird has landed on my windowsill and watched me getting dressed in the morning. I do not know who lost it, but it allows me to touch it and pet its feathers. When I am ready to leave, it flies off, and then it returns at night to watch me prepare for bed. It is the most precious thing I have ever seen."

When the king heard this he roared with anger. "Guards!" he exclaimed. He paused and then spoke to the princess. "Daughter, I hate to tell you this, but I am at war with a druid. He came here demanding payment for cutting into his forest. HIS FOREST! I am the king. All forests are mine! The nerve of the man! When I called for his head, he turned into a small songbird and flew away. I thought I was rid of him. Now I find that he has been watching my own daughter dress and undress every morning and night. I will have his head and burn down his forest. So what if we inadvertently destroyed his home. He was not given permission to live there."

The princess said, "Oh my. How long did he live there before you found out?"

The king said, "I am told thousands of years."

The princess looked perplexed. "Then, Father, he was here before our ancestors. He has a right to his land."

The king was not interested. "I own that land. I own all land. I am not in a sharing mood! Do you know what he wanted for payment?"

"No."

"You. My own daughter. It seems he has been interested in you for some time, and now he has been spying on your bedchamber."

She blushed red while pretending anger and asked, "Why would he be watching me each day? He must have received his eyeful by now. What will you do?"

The guards came, and the king gave orders. The king said, "Druids cannot change shape if they don't have the room to change into their own form. I will have him captured and placed into a tiny little cage with no door." Then his smile turned deeper and he said, "I will let you keep him forever as a little bird. Think of the joy his songs will give you and the frustration he will go through seeing you every day and never being allowed to touch you. A magical cage that will make him sing happily but will also keep him frustrated at the close proximity of the girl he apparently loves. What a fitting punishment it will be when he sees you wed to a proper husband. Each morning and night, he will see and know that he can never have you." He looked away and shouted, "Wizard!"

The wizard came into the room and said, "Yes, Majesty."

"I need a cage for a very small bird. One with no door and impossible to break. I need it magically fixed so that any bird in the cage will be forced to sing happily."

The old wizard said, "I have a friend that has an artifact cage like that. It is very small. Too small for a normal bird, but a small bird should fit. It would have no place to spread its wings. It would be cramped and uncomfortable. It was used for a pixie that got too full of itself. The happy singing spell is easy. I assure you the cage cannot open unless the bird dies of natural causes."

The king smiled. "Perfect!"

The wizard said, "I shall make it happen."

The king turned to his daughter. "Keep the bird happy until the cage is ready."

The daughter said, with an evil grin, "I will, Father."

That night, when the bird showed up in the princess's window, she gave it extra attention, ensuring it saw her change into her night clothes and slide into bed across silk sheets. The bird flew around the bed several times before leaving.

Two days later the cage was ready. The wizard handed it to the princess with verbal instructions. "Just touch this cage to the bird and it will instantly be inside. Are you sure you want to do this? The bird will never get out as the spells are very powerful. It will always act happy. The cage is made of an unbreakable material. It will never escape."

The princess took the cage and kissed the cheek of the wizard and left. That night, the princess held the cage behind her back as the little bird flew in and started singing. She walked up to it and touched the cage to the bird, and it vanished, only to reappear inside the cage. At first it was in panic, but then the spell took effect and it started to happily sing. She put the cage down and prepared for bed. The bird tried to fly, tried to get out, but the cage held. It was still singing, but it was obviously agitated. The bird was breathing hard from its escape efforts and acting like it wanted out more than anything.

The princess bent down and said to the little bird, "Well, Princess, thanks to the king I have you caged, and when I kill your father, I will become him, and I will be in charge of my lands again."

# The Hand of God

The fight lasted only a little time, but the outcome was devastating. The cleric was dead, and so was the wizard. Three of the orcs surrendered and dropped their weapons. The paladin was shocked at the carnage and just stood there acting paralyzed. I tried to kill the three prisoners, but the paladin would not allow it. His code forbade that he allow harm to come to unarmed creatures.

I took another shot at the lead orc with the double scar running down the left side of his face, but the paladin stepped in the way and took the arrow on his shield, yelling, "Cease, rogue! You will not harm these orcs. He said to the orcs, "You may go if you give me your word you will leave and never return and that you will not harm another human."

They groveled and said, "You have our word. We will leave and not return, and we will leave the humans alone."

"Then go."

They left, and I said to the paladin, "Fool! Of course they will not return. Everyone here is dead. Look at the pot. They were cooking the children of this village. They eat our children, and you let them go on a promise you know they will never keep!"

The paladin answered, saying, "I wonder about you sometimes, rogue. If you are of goodly nature, as you claim, then why do you have evil thoughts? How could you possibly consider taking the life of someone that surrendered? How could you stab someone that is without weapon? You are but a common thief. You are no rogue."

The lady barbarian said, "We are in a situation here, gentlemen. We cannot afford the time to take prisoners, and killing unarmed combatants is not approved by our leader."

I said, "I never voted to allow the paladin control of anything, and now his folly will be the death of more innocent women and children. Mark my word on that. If it happens, I will not cease. I will kill the paladin if necessary, but I will not let such monsters go."

The paladin said, "If we did not need you so badly, rogue, I would ask you to leave this party. Try to kill another unarmed combatant and I will send you home bleeding."

I said, "If the king had not commanded it of me, I would have never joined up with a fool paladin. Do not worry, child who knows not his god's will. I will leave the moment I am allowed—the moment my portion of this kingly request is fulfilled."

The paladin was in shock and enraged at my reference to his god. He took a swing at me, and I leaned into it so that I would take the full power of his gauntleted fist. I had no weapon out. I raised no hand to him. I took the hit and fell back ten feet. I stood up, and after using a wand to heal my shattered jaw, I said, "Hypocrite. You let murderers go that eat our children simply because they dropped their weapons, but you would harm someone of your own party that raised no hand against you but does not agree with your views. Again I say, hypocrite." I walked away to check if anyone was alive.

The barbarian asked, "Rogue, can you do anything to help the cleric?"

I answered snidely, saying, "I will try if the paladin requires it of me. After all, you put the charlatan in charge. I feel sorry for his god and for us. First, we need to attend any wounded before they meet the same fate."

The paladin said, "I so order it."

The paladin and barbarian started looking through the carnage, but there were no villagers alive. No women, children, dogs, or cats. Everything was dead except the three of us, and personally I could think of another that deserved death a lot more than these villagers. I returned to the cleric and pulled out a scroll. I was always good at using magic devices. I can use any wand and most rods. Scrolls are tricky sometimes, and this was a powerful scroll. I said to the barbarian, "I am going to try a Resurrection scroll, so please stand back. If something goes wrong, I don't want the two of you harmed."

The paladin said, "You may want to pray to God before you use that scroll. Sobelli may not be happy with you after your careless and foolish words."

I said, "No problem, charlatan. I have only one tool from Sobelli, and it is not a scroll. This is a scroll from a god that has champions that are goodly in nature. I feel sorry for the grand god Sobelli being stuck with the likes of you." The rage of the paladin was palpable, but he dared not do anything as long as the scroll was out and being used. Even he was not that big a fool. I opened up the scroll and concentrated. I did say a prayer to the goddess Dimidims, the goddess of halflings, before using her scroll. It took a little longer than it would for a cleric of Dimidims, but she knew my heart was true, and the cleric's eyes opened.

The cleric asked, "What happened? I was flanking an orc, and then I was floating in paradise. Now I am back here smelling blood and gore."

I was about to answer when I was lifted off the ground where I was kneeling and turned to face an angry paladin. I did not fight back. I said, "I surrender."

The paladin slammed me up against a tree, cracking several tree limbs and several ribs. "I will not have you talking about me in that manner. I cannot have you usurping my power as leader." His face was only inches from mine, and his breath was to choke on. "Do you understand, rogue?"

I said, "I understand, friend of evil, orc lover, charlatan."

He dropped me and turned to the cleric, saying, "The wizard is down. Please do what you can to bring him up. We have a long way to go, and we will need that heathen spell-slinger."

I thought to myself, *Anyone who does not worship Sobelli is a heathen to this paladin. All other gods are blasphemous. All other points of view are discouraged with fist and sword.*

The cleric said, "I cannot do anything today. We will have to wait until tomorrow so that I can pray for the correct spell."

The paladin said, "Rogue, do you have any more of those heathen scrolls?"

I said, "I do, but they are for returning the cleric to life so that he can return us to life."

"We will use one now."

I concentrated on what to say, as this was going to spin him up more and we did not need that. "I am sorry, but no, we will not. I will be saving them for the reason stated. The cleric knows I have them and how to get to them in emergencies. Having the wizard alive today is not an emergency."

The paladin said, "I did not ask. It is an order."

"I do not take orders from you. That scroll is not party treasure. You told us we would not be reimbursed for consumables, such as scrolls, wands, and potions. A Resurrection scroll costs over ten thousand gold, and a second scroll is not for wasting. In another matter, the king did not put you in charge, and neither did I. If I recall correctly, the king said, and I quote, 'Work it out among you, but be careful, as a zealot is not a good choice.' There is only one zealot among us, and that is you. Therefore, by the king's own words, you are the only one not qualified, in my opinion. I vote for the barbarian. She is far more intelligent and capable in battle.

She knows the meaning of retreat, tactics, not leaving an enemy behind you to tell others, and not running in without a plan. She knows what sneak attack means, that surprise is important, and that sometimes hiding is a good choice."

He started toward me but stopped when the cleric stepped in front of him. "I take it I missed something. The two of you did not say three words to each other for over a week, and now your hate has come to full bloom. I am surprised at the rogue and disappointed with you, paladin."

The paladin turned on the cleric, saying, "Out of my way, heathen worshiper. I have had enough of this rogue. I will put an end to it. You can resurrect it later. Right now I am going to beat him to death."

I took a Fly potion from my pack and drank it as he yelled at the cleric. Then I said, "If we battle, you will require the help of the cleric, wizard, and barbarian. You are too big a coward to fight me on your own resources."

The paladin, being named a coward, flew into a rage, turned back to the cleric, and yelled, "No help. Hear that, cleric. You will give no help to either of us." He turned back to me and said, "We shall let Sobelli determine who is correct in their views. If I am right, and I am, Sobelli will ensure I win. If you are correct, then Sobelli will not help me. Prepare to die, rogue."

I said as I pulled my bow, "If I win this battle, then you will willingly give up being the leader in favor of the barbarian. You will obey her in all things during this assignment, and you will admit that you are wrong. You have already said that your god will help you if you are right and will not help you if you are wrong. I cannot win against your god, but if you are wrong in your views and it is truly one-on-one, then I will win and you will admit that you do not know your god's will regarding how to treat friends and enemies."

The paladin said, "Done. If I win, I will have you resurrected, and you will obey me in everything and pray to my god. If you win, I will obey the barbarian in everything and pray for enlightenment. You understand that you have no chance." He dropped his shield and took his sword in two hands, saying, "Ready to die, rogue?"

I flew up twenty feet and said, "Ready."

He yelled in rage, as he had no Fly potions. He had told the wizard to keep several Fly spells ready for need, but he had not seen the need to waste money on potions for spells the wizard and cleric should know and use. Arrogant fool. I pulled out a wand of Lightning Bolt and blasted him.

He yelled while smoking a little, "Come down here, coward!"

I yelled back, "This is a wand of Lightning Bolt made by a wizard that worshipped Sobelli. A rare thing that is. It is the only item of Sobelli I own. If Sobelli wants you to allow killers to go free, then this wand will not work." I struck him with lighting five more times, and I would swear the lightning bent to ensure it hit him. Sobelli was watching. The paladin tried everything to get to me, but he was not prepared and his god was not helping him. He prayed, and I hit him with another lightning bolt. His armor was melting in several places. He tried to use his healing abilities, but his god refused to allow it. He tried a spell, but it did not work, so he fell to his knees and said, "I surrender and freely give up. I will comply with my word. My god has forsaken me in this, and I know I am wrong."

I floated down and said, "I accept."

He grabbed me and said, "Now I have you, and now you will die!"

Instantly I was twenty feet above him. I do not know how, unless Sobelli did it. No one in the party had the ability, except maybe the wizard, but he was still dead. My hand came up, and the wand pointed. I had dropped the wand when the paladin grabbed me, but now it was in my hand again. I said the trigger word, and all the lightning bolts left in the wand emerged at the same time, destroying the wand and leaving only a deep hole where the paladin had been kneeling. I fell to my knees and prayed to Sobelli for forgiveness.

What I received in return for my prayer was, "Do not try to resurrect that charlatan. Wait there; a true paladin is on his way." We all heard it, including the wizard, who was now standing there, looking at the hole in confusion. The cleric was on his knees, as was I. The barbarian was standing there looking into the sky with tears. She said, "Did you see it? Did you see the hand of God?"

# A Low-Level Party (Fighter)

I stepped into the adventuring bar and looked around. Even though I had been dreaming about this all my life, I had no idea who to talk to or what to do. I went to the bar and sat down on an empty stool, taking extra care not to upset any of the people there. All were far above me. I recognized Falin the Falcon in the corner with his friends. There was Thomas of the Missing Eye group. His entire group was partying in the center of the tavern, and they had a feast fit for a king on the main table. I was just starting to think I was in the wrong place when the bartender asked if I was thirsty.

"Yes, sir. A beer, please."

"Coming right up, young master."

He placed the beer in front of me, and I sipped it while watching the rest of the people. The bartender watched me for a while, and then I think he took pity on the new graduate from the fighters' school. "Looking for a little adventure, mate?"

I must have looked frightened and nearly ready to leave as he smiled and placed a hand on my shoulder, saying, "Then you're in the right place."

I said, "Sir, I think I am way over my head."

"Nonsense. See that big board over there?" He pointed to a board on the far wall. "All you need to do is walk over to that wall and start reading the postings. Someone will come to you. These people will know what skills you have graduated with. But come and see me before you decide on any one group. I will let you know if you are getting in over your head. I have been doing this for twenty years, and I seldom make a mistake. I like repeat customers, so keeping you alive and growing in your skills is important to me. You just walk over and start reading. You can read, can't you?"

"Four different languages."

"Good then."

I stood up and started to cross the room. The bartender said, "Leave the beer, boy. Trying to carry it around the room will get you into trouble."

I set the beer down and made my way across the overly crowded room. I was bumped into at least ten times. I was very glad I did not have that beer in hand. Apologizing was bad enough, but apologizing to someone I had gotten wet would possibly have cost me my life. The board was filled with all kinds of requests for help. One, in exceptional handwriting and fancy scroll, I instantly liked. It said simply, "Need highly experienced fighter for travel into the abyss. See Cosmos for details."

That's all it said, and I loved it. I found my finger touching the side and running down it like it was gold. I jerked it away. I wanted so badly to apply right then, but knew I would be killed instantly if they were fools enough to accept me—and I doubted that they were; fools don't live long in this profession. They taught me a lot at the Fighter's Guild, and one thing that stuck in my mind and came out right then was the saying "There are old fighters and bold fighters, but few old bold fighters." It's a cliché that probably everyone knows. That does not make it any less true. The next post was a little more down-to-earth.

"We're making a trip into the city sewers to kill a rat problem. This city has big rats. Anyone interested, raise your hand."

This was not my idea of a style—if I would ever actually get a style. It was more a guardsman's job, and a smelly one at that. A man in full plate walked up to me and said, "I started out cleaning sewers and anything else I could do to gain experience, boy. Swallow your pride and raise your hand."

I looked at him eye-to-eye and flinched in respect. The great Falcon himself. All I could manage was "Yes, sir." I raised my hand. He walked back over to his group, and they acted like nothing had happened, but I would remember this all my life. The great Falcon gave me advice, and I took it.

A woman came up to me and asked, "Interested in cleaning sewers, young man?"

I said, "Yes, my lady."

"Then follow me." She led me over to a table with four other people, all looking a little scared under false looks of bravado. She introduced us. "This is Mathew. He is a new graduate of the Wizard's Academy. This is Sister Patty of the Church of Sobelli. This is Buddy, a graduate from the Rogue Academy. He is trying to find a new name, but right now he goes by Silent. Expect that to change. This is Richard, a fellow fighter and recent graduate of the guild."

Richard and I clasped hands and slapped each other on the back. We had spent many days together practicing and knew each other well. The others shook hands, and I sat down.

The lady said, "I know that this is not what was in your hearts and dreams when you joined your prospective professions, but please believe me when I say that this is where you should start. Your group is assigned by the city to clean out the sewers of all creatures. That means rats, stray dogs, alligators, or any animal you find. Now listen to me well. If you run into something you cannot handle, then leave the sewers. Mark the place where it was last seen, write down anything about it you can, report it to the watch captain so he can handle it, and start working a different part of the sewers until the captain says it's all right to go back in. You are not expendable. I have a dozen jobs for you to do, and each one gets progressively harder. This is just the first. Do it well, become a cohesive group, and make me proud, and those other jobs are yours. You have two days to prepare before reporting into the main watch. The sewers are big, and you could be down there for weeks without seeing an exit. The watch captain will give you a map. It is up to you to figure out where you are. The map will be waiting for you at the watch captain's desk."

I asked, "Why two days? We could start tomorrow."

The lady smiled. "I need two days to get permission from the Thieves' Guild to allow you safe passage. Do not attack any thieves. Don't report on them. Say nothing about them. I want your sworn word on this."

We all gave her our word.

The lady continued. "Good then. Prepare, and be waiting at the main watch tower at first light two days hence. I have secured you a room for two days in this tavern. Your pay will be room and board plus twenty gold a day each." She stood and left.

I looked at the others, and though I did not feel it myself, I put enthusiasm into my voice as I made introductions and told them about myself. I listened carefully about each of the others and noted some prejudice in the wizard and the cleric. They did not like rogues. Considered them thieves. Also, the cleric was upset that none of the rest of us worshipped her god.

I said, "I can only thank the gods that we have a rogue. He will be trained in finding traps and following underground maps. It is a big place, and I do not feel like getting lost and starving to death in a sewer." I looked at the rogue and asked, "You can follow a map without getting turned around or lost?"

"I have some skill in that, but I am just a beginner at being a rogue. I can find traps if I am allowed to take my time in doing so. Disabling them is far more difficult."

I said, "If you can find them, then we don't die instantly. Traps can be nasty, and the gods know we need your skills. If it looks like a difficult trap to disable, then we will mark it on the map and work around it somehow." I looked at the rest of them and saw they were starting to warm up to the rogue. I said, "We will be underground. Everyone will need light of some sort and food for three weeks."

The wizard, a little boy compared to the rest of us, said, "Light I can create; food will weigh me down. I have a backpack, but I cannot carry much more than a few days' worth of rations. Torches are completely out of the question."

I said, "You figure out what you need, and the rest of us will help carry some of it. We have limits also, so only bring what you need."

The cleric said, "I will not carry someone else's stuff. I do not have room."

I said, "We will determine what everyone will carry tomorrow night. We have a room here. Gather what you need and meet me in our room tomorrow night for discussions on tactics. I do not want to lose anyone on this trip."

The wizard and cleric stood up and left. The rogue looked at me in a funny way and then said, "You will make a good leader." Then he left.

I looked at Richard and said, "Let's return to the guild and obtain advice on what we will need and what to expect. The better prepared we are, the better chance we have of coming out alive."

Richard said, while using his hands to show eight or nine inches, "It's only rats."

I smiled. "Rats come in sizes from small to bigger than humans, and the lady said they have a *big* rat problem. Besides, they carry disease. Alligators are good at hiding and attacking when you least expect it. Also, there are rumors that there is something killing off anyone who enters. We are being hired as bait. I want to turn that around to us being scouts." I could see he did not understand, so I added, "When you have something big killing and eating everything, how do you bring it out into the open?"

Richard thought for a second. "Got me. How?"

I smiled. Richard was a good fighter but not too good on tactics. "Send someone in to kill off all the food. No matter that the ones sent in will end up being the only food left."

Richard's eyes opened wide. "That lady hired us as bait?"

I nearly laughed. "Yes. Why do you think she is paying so much? She doesn't think we will be collecting. Let's talk to old Master Godfree. Let's turn it around on her."

Richard said, "I'm with you."

We stood to leave, but others pushed us down. The Searchers surrounded us, and one sat down across from me and said, "Couldn't help but overhear your speech to the others, boy. Good start. Pull them together. Make then realize they need each other. Start them understanding that each has his weakness and will need help. And plan. Very good start, boy. I am impressed, and that is not easy to do. We will all be watching your group."

I said, "Thank you, sir."

He smiled. "And you are polite to your betters, boy. That will get you far."

I smiled. "Thank you, sir, but if my father ever found out I was not polite, he would hunt me down and tan my hide in front of anyone who happened to be present."

They all laughed. "We know what you are about to go through, and we think you are right. You see, that lady hired us to take out the creatures you can't handle. However, we get paid by the creature, and therefore we are hoping that you report often and find a lot of creatures you can't handle. So, some advice before you go. See this Godfree friend of yours. Plan out your route, and let us know which exits you are going to come out of. That way we can have someone waiting at the exits. They will gather the group, and you can show us personally. That will make it easier on you and us."

"Yes, sir. Please don't take offense at what I am about to say, but I feel you deserve the truth."

"Go ahead, boy."

"We can plan that into our daily routine, but I cannot take your advice until I check with the captain to ensure you are actually telling us the truth. I know your reputation, and I trust you and your group, but you may have a hidden agenda."

"You do that, boy. In fact, I plan on being there for your briefing. You have a good head on your shoulders. Try to keep it there." They got up and left. All were laughing.

We made it to the Guild without another incident and found Godfree in the study.

Godfree exclaimed, "Back so soon! What? Getting hungry and can't find work?"

We sat down with him and talked about the contract and made plans half the night. I was surprised at the things we would need to do.

"First, no metal armor. It's wet and cold down there, and your father's full plate will be rusted before the first day is out. Go down to the storeroom and pull out a couple of leather jerkins and thick high-top leather boots and tar the boots to waterproof them. Second, it's dark down there. That fool wizard wants to use light spells and use up all his spells before getting into battle. Fool boy. You take as many torches as possible and, if you can afford it, a couple of magic glow rods for emergencies. We taught you how to make a torch, boy. You take only two poles each and all the soaked rags you can carry. That will give you more room and less weight. Use as little light as possible. One or two torches at a time should be plenty, as your eyes will adjust. Don't you carry them. You make the cleric and wizard carry them so that your hands are free for pulling your shield and sword. If you are carrying them and need both hands, then you have to drop the torch or pass it off. If you drop it, the sewer water will put it out instantly, and then you're fighting in the dark. Third, distribute the provisions between you. Don't carry all the food or torches in one pack. That pack gets destroyed, you're in deep trouble. Fourth, use your nose. If it starts to smell like a giant torch, then the air is holding methane. Your torch will light the methane and set you all on fire. You can't breathe in that either, so don't go in. Mark it on your map and go around or find a spot where you can shoot a fire arrow into the area without getting caught in the fire."

"Yes, sir."

Godfree also said, "I know the Searchers. Good people all. You work with them and learn. Do not fight something you have no idea about or that you find out is more difficult than you thought. Pull back, regroup, and seek advice from the Searchers. They will probably know what it was you tried to fight and will either tell you its weakness, if it is below them, or come help take it out and collect their part of the funding for this job. Still, you can learn from either."

After that we talked long about the weaknesses and strengths of the creatures we may find down there. We talked about useful potions and not wasting potions. We were to use renewable resources, such as spells, for healing. We would talk to the captain about circumstances like becoming diseased and what to do about them. His last words were, "Do not go into a situation you cannot handle. Stay alive and well boys, and bring back the rest of your party intact."

He stood up, and we exchanged handshakes and pats. Just before we parted, he said something he always said that had never really sunk in before, but it struck home this time. "Never leave anyone behind."

That was three years ago. Now our group of adventurers are the ones partying in the Inn. I watched as a young boy left his drink on the bar and tripped his way to the board. I smiled when his fingers touched the note our wizard had posted. I waited until I was sure he had read all the posts, and then I stood up and walked over. People got out of my way, leaving a path to the trembling young man. He tried to look so brave, but his voice trembled and his hands were sweating. I said, "I started out cleaning sewers and anything else I could do to gain experience, boy. Swallow your pride and raise your hand." I walked back to our little group. No one said a word. I did not need to look. I knew that boy had raised his hand.

# The Rogue: Party of Six (High Level)

I walked into the room, and no one noticed. I took the seat by the fire with my back to the wall, and it was minutes before I allowed the serving wench to see me and she came over.

"Something to drink, my lord?"

"Wine."

"We have several kinds of wines, my lord, ranging from two copper a bottle all the way up to two hundred gold a glass."

"Your best wine, the entire bottle, and one clean glass."

Her eyes widened, and she nearly tripped as she headed to the bar.

"Bud, the one in the corner wants our best wine. The entire bottle."

The bartender looked at me for the first time. He looked at my clothes and shoes but saw nothing special—an average man, wearing average clothes, on a normal night. He came out from behind his bar with a war hammer hanging from his side. He was short, even for his dwarven race, but he more than made up for it in girth. He was as wide as two men and probably as strong.

As he came closer, I could see he was dirty and smelly. The rag hanging from his arm was dirtier than he, and his beard had food in it from a week ago and had never seen a brush. "I'm told you want a bottle of my finest wine. What are you paying with?"

A two-thousand-gold-piece platinum bar instantly appeared in my hand. I placed it on the table and whispered, in a threatening voice, "The bottle better not be watered down."

He picked up the platinum bar, weighed it in his hand, smelled it, and then bit it nearly in two. "Done." He turned and left.

The wench returned with a bottle of wine worth maybe half what I had paid, so I said, "Tell the dwarf that I said if he wants to live, he had better have better wine than that or return my platinum bar intact. And I said a *clean* glass."

The wench's eyes turned scared, and she took the bottle and glass back to the bar. The Dwarf roared with anger but quickly calmed down and reluctantly pulled out another bottle and handed it to the wench, saying, "Be careful with that, child. It's worth more than your entire family."

She brought the wine over and gently put it on the table and then went quickly to the kitchen and came out with another glass. She set it down in front of me, and I tipped her one platinum. She picked it up with trembling hands, and it disappeared as she curtsied and said, "Thank you, my lord." She returned to work the crowd, leaving me with a clean glass and a bottle of very good elvin wine. I sat and waited, sipping slowly and watching everything.

Eventually they came in—the party that had put up the notice. "Highly Experienced Rogue Needed: If you don't mind a little adventure underground, would like to make a fistful of gold, and can work well in a team, then be here waiting for us on the night of the first moon of spring." Typical sales pitch for a dangerous mission. Any beginner rogue and many young rogues would pass up that message. Spelunking can be fun, but you don't want to get in over your head. Still, there were five other rogues waiting in the bar. Two were fools that would not last out the day on a high-level mission. One was an old, experienced human that would do well, but he would be slow and less alert; humans lose something when they reach the age of sixty. Two were possible competition: a dwarf from Iron Mountain that knew the undergrounds and would do well in this environment, and a half-dragon from the isles. She would do well also. Her training came from the best, and she had proven herself many times. We exchanged hand signs, letting each other know we were not hostile.

The party that walked in sat down at a large table. There was a cleric, a sorcerer, two fighters, and a surprise. It had been a long time since I had seen a druid. I knew this druid. We had worked together over three hundred years ago.

I let myself fade into the wall so that I would not be noticed so quickly. This was indeed a very high-ranking party, and therefore the goal would be extremely dangerous. The fighter was one of the king's hands, licensed to do anything he wanted without recourse. He was the king's law; he could kill a baron, and only the king could call him on it. The other fighter was unknown to me but looked very capable and had mithril full plate with twin battle axes on his back, and he carried everything like it weighed nothing and was part of his body. The sorcerer was known. He was a coward that lived because he left. In so doing, he would leave the others to fight without an arcane spell caster. The sorcerer was capable and could sling some nasty spells, but if the fight got to him, he would leave by teleporting out. The cleric I had also heard of. A father of the Red Hand, worshiper of Ultio, and—when sober—a great help with undead. He was also a mean fighter with that magical three-headed artifact morningstar. The druid, Espial, had been my good friend and lover long ago, until she left me for another. That was the best time of my life and the worst. It would be difficult working with her. Still, it was easy to see that they were lacking a rogue, range fighting, and healing. The cleric was a fighter and seldom used healing during battle except on himself, and Espial was more into turning to bird form and attacking with spells from above. A good rogue can use magic devices like wands of healing, and I could use any wand ever made.

One of the fools approached the party. "Good day, sirs and madam."

The king's hand said, "Good day to you, sir. How may I be of assistance?

"I am told that you may be in need of the services of a rogue. I am such a person, and I happen to be in between positions at the moment."

The fighter motioned for him to take a seat. "So, you deem yourself a rogue. We are going up against the Mantling Sisters and their underground network. Do you think you can get us safely through all the traps?"

The fool stood up and said, "No, sir. I cannot do that. That is suicide for any rogue."

He left, and so did the other rogue fool, who suddenly realized he was way out of his league. I snorted, and the druid looked in my direction but saw nothing, and that raised her curiosity. Still, being professional, she remained sitting and looked elsewhere.

The human turned away and looked into his cup as if to say, "Not for me." The dwarf from Iron Mountain stood up and said, "I can lead you through the sisters' traps and help fight while doing so."

The fighter motioned for him to attend the party of adventures. "Good dwarf, I am glad to see you do not flinch at such a task. The amount of undead is daunting even for our cleric. It seems the sisters have a pet lich." They talked for a little while, but at one point the dwarf stood up and said, "I am sorry, but this is not my fight." He turned and left.

The female half-dragon stood up and left also. She had listened the same as I and knew she was no match for this party. I watched as they had dinner. I sipped my wine and called the serving wench over. "Send the rest of this bottle to that table, and give this note to the druid female." -

She took the wine and the note. She placed the wine on their table while pointing to me, but she became confused, as she could not see me. She handed the note to Espial. She read it out loud, as I knew she would. "Hello, Espial. After three hundred years, you haven't changed."

She looked all around for me, saying to her friends in a whisper, "The Rogue! He is here."

The fighter stood up and drew his sword, and people scrambled out of his way; many left. "What rogue? Are we in trouble? You seem in a panic."

She said, "The Rogue. Three hundred years ago, I was in a party that cleared the Handless Tower. We would have never made it if not for the Rogue. I am not in a panic. He was my lover until I left him for another. I tossed him out after I no longer needed him. It was in my younger days. I was a fool."

I said into her ear, just loud enough for the others to hear, "Yes, you were."

She turned, but I had already moved into hiding.

She said, "Rogue! Stop playing games with us."

I stood right next to the fighter and asked, "Why? It is very easy," before disappearing again. There were many shadows in the room, and it was easy to hide.

The fighter said, "Your rogue has a sense of humor."

Espial said, "He is not my rogue. No one can own him. He is as free as the wind and harder to catch. He let me have him in my hands once, and I let him go. It was a mistake."

The fighter asked, "What is this rogue's name?"

Espial said, in tears, "He has no name. He needs no name. He is the Rogue."

The fighter said, "Rogue! I would have words with you. Show yourself."

I was standing right next to the cleric when I said, "And what words would you have with me, fighter? I take it you are the leader of this young band of misfits."

The fighter looked at me with a smile. "Hello, elf. We are known as the King's Talon. I am Daniel, the cleric is Father Norton, the sorcerer is called Orper, and this fighter is called Grinder. You seem to know our druid, Espial."

I smiled and said, "I know, or have heard of most of you. I am the Rogue."

The fighter said, "Please have a seat. We are looking for a good rogue."

I stopped him, saying, "Please don't give me that crap about the Mantling Sisters and their underground network. I cleaned that out two years ago, and the king knows, and therefore you know."

The entire party was now paying great attention as the fighter asked, "What party did you take in?"

"No party."

The fighter frowned. "Who were you with? How many died?"

"I went in alone, and I did not die; though I came very close on several occasions."

The cleric said, "I think we have found our rogue."

The sorcerer asked, "You actually believe this fool?"

My dirk was out and I was sitting in the sorcerer's lap with the blade to his throat before he could move. The sorcerer always used a contingency to teleport away or had an orb of protection surround him if he was physically attacked. Because I was sitting in lap, his contingency would include me, and therefore he could not escape. His contingency was the orb, and I was inside with him. I slit his throat from ear to ear and then stabbed him over and over until he was dead. The others were trying to get to me and stop me, but the sorcerer's own spell prevented them. When he died, the spell dissipated. The fighter's blade was now at my throat. I paid it no attention as I cleaned my blade on the sorcerer's cape and sheathed it.

Espial asked, "Before you die, would you please explain why you just killed our sorcerer?"

I said, "Just a moment." I took out a stone I had acquired a few decades ago and touched it to the sorcerer's head, and he was instantly resurrected. He would remember the pain I just put him through. He would never forget what being cut to death feels like. I said, "Orper, do you know why I did that?"

Orper was in fear and had a difficult time talking as his hand was feeling for the cut in his throat that was no longer there. The fighter asked, "I doubt he does. I would like to know." He sheathed his blade.

I said, "Orper took a party to the lich queen's lair. When things heated up, they were all supposed to teleport out. They ran at Orper so that they could leave, but Orper panicked and left without them. It is not the first time he has done this. Two in the party were my friends. I had to go in and clean up the mess he left behind. My two friends were turned into wraiths. I had to cut them to bits to kill them." I looked over at Espial and then at the tabletop. "It was the first time I have cried in three hundred years." Then my face turned very serious as I looked directly into Orper's eyes and said, "I have been looking for you, Orper, to give you this message. If it happens again, I will find you and do things to you that will make you wish you had not chickened out. Do you understand, coward?"

Orper said with a shaky voice, "I … I understand."

The fighter looked at the others and said, "This we did not know about our sorcerer. We cannot have this in the party. Not where we are going."

Father Norton said, "Orper, it is time for you to retire to some kingdom and play house sorcerer to some noble. If you flee at the first sign of danger, then you are the danger and it will get you killed." He looked at me and added, "Again."

The other fighter said, "Flee when we finally need you and I will hunt you down personally. It would be better if you left now."

Orper stood up. "Retirement sounds very good right now. I always wanted to be a sage, and I have a tower to manage that I have neglected far too long. I am sorry, but I cannot be with you at this time." He teleported away.

I said, "I have completed what I have come to do." I stood back up.

The fighter quickly asked, "Did you do that to warn the sorcerer or to save Espial?"

I took a glimpse at my old friend. "I did not know she was in this party. When I found out a moment ago, I had to struggle with whether or not to leave Orper dead so that he could not harm her. As you can see, I kept with the plan."

Espial said, "We need you, Rogue. The kingdom is at stake. Tens of thousands will die if we do not succeed."

I smiled. "Nothing new there. Something is always causing this catastrophe or that disaster. I have spent many years stopping, postponing, or trimming down the effects of just such issues."

The fighter said, "The Lord of Obscurity is loose."

My eyes must have narrowed and my face must have shown my hatred as the fighter said, "You have met him before, Rogue?"

I said, "Once. Our group stopped him at great cost, and we had a chance to destroy him, but the leader of our band decided to imprison him in his own tower. The Wiz and I begged to be allowed to destroy him, but the fool paladin would not kill something we had made helpless. Now you tell me he is loose and powerful again. I am displeased."

Espial said, "Yes, and we are tasked to destroy him. There will not be any imprisonment this time. He has forfeited his right to life."

I asked, "Is this agreed upon by all?"

The fighter said, "It is the king's order, and we have checked with our gods, and it is agreed on by all."

"I will be right back." I disappeared. Shortly I returned with an elvin wizard in tow.

Wiz said, "I am told my sworn enemy is loose and causing trouble again and that you want him destroyed. I'm in."

The fighter said, "Then prepare for travel by land and sea. We have a ways to go to reach his new hiding place."

The Wiz said, "I will return to this spot in two days. I will be ready."

I said, "I am always ready."

Espial sprouted a wicked smile as she took my hand and said, "Yes, you always were."

We found the old enemy and totally destroyed him. Wasn't that difficult with this group. The king made us the "Right Hand of the King," and now we ride the land administering his law and correcting issues that barons, dukes, and the army cannot handle. Today we are off to put down a gargantuan ancient evil dragon that is setting fire to ships and port towns on our western coast. Minor little issue that won't take long.

# The Ranger

I love this hill. It's a great place to watch the town and see if there are any morons trying to take shortcuts through the woods. The road leading west winds continuously and often cuts back on itself. If a person knows the woods, he or she can cut the travel time from here to the city by weeks, avoid all the bandits, and save on the cost of supplies. Yesterday, I was in the town, spreading the idea that taking the shortcuts would save time and money but would also be very dangerous. Even though I emphasized *dangerous*, no one said a thing, like normal. They believe they can cut through the woods without help.

Ah look, four adventurers leaving the city, and they are not taking the road. If they would have hired me yesterday, I would have charged much less than what I will charge after they are helplessly lost. I know, it's not very nice taking advantage of them like that, but aren't they trying to take advantage of me? It was my idea, and I did mention that anyone wanting to go that route needed my help and that I would be happy to provide it for a modest fee. Yet there they are, subverting my business by going it alone. Fools all, and it will cost them.

I climbed down from the tree and onto the back of my horse. Good horse, Tom. I paid little for him, as he is not fast and not good looking, but he is strong and can walk forever across any terrain, as sure-footed as a mountain goat. Once, he chased a large higer across

Needle Point Pass. He would have killed that six-footed, double-fanged cat if not for my stopping him. Fool cat should have known better than try to eat a horse like Tom. Got him stomped good and then chased for eighteen leagues across the steepest, most dangerous terrain in the mountains.

I pointed Tom in the right direction. I was going to the next peak to see which way they'd get themselves lost. There are lots of ways to get lost in the forest. Following a path will always get you lost. The ones making the path, normally deer, moose, dorcals, and bears, tend to go around in circles in their own little territories. Another is the follow-the-sun method. Soon the forest will not allow the sun in. What then? And the sun moves, so you continuously change direction. Pick out a mountain peak. That will get you there, but is "there" a good place to be, and do you know where the pass is? Most are difficult to find, and without the knowledge, it could take you months to find the pass. My favorite is the It's-in-that-direction method. After traveling in circles, they usually find themselves back at the town about three days later. The ones I was currently watching looked like a pick-a-mountain-peak group. I made it to the next peak, set up camp, and waited. It would be days before they made it that far. Sure enough, two days later, just about sundown, they showed up. It was difficult to make them out from that height, but the noise they were making made it easy to find them. I caught only bits and pieces of the argument as it rang throughout the mountains. However, it was enough to figure out they were lost already. Amateurs!

I climbed back on Tom and headed down the mountain to intercept the little adventuring party. It was just after dark when I found them. They were following a trail. I was wrong about this group; they were worse than amateurs. They did not bring netting for the bugs; they had food out, just waiting for predators; and they could not find water for cooking. I sat back in the saddle and listened.

"Rogue, find us some water!"

"How am I supposed to do that, Carl? I was hired on as a rogue, not a scout. I have never been in a forest like this in all my life, and I have no idea where water is."

Carl was apparently the fighter and, for some reason that I will never understand, seemed to be in charge.

Carl said, "Cleric, you can make food and water, can't you?"

The cleric said, "I can purify it, but I cannot create it. I am not that powerful. I don't even know if there is a spell for such. And don't ask me to go looking. I would be lost in a second in the dark. I am from the city, not the country. This assignment was for the city, and I cannot be of assistance with this current issue."

The wizard looked over at the fighter and said, "I will cast Find the Path to get us out of the forest tomorrow. Be warned, the path may take us back to the town or even farther away. Wording the request will be difficult, as I have no idea how to word it. I, too, have never been in the woods before."

The fighter said, "We need to be in the city in two weeks. Going back to the town of Four Corners would be a bad mistake. Using the road will take six weeks at best."

The rogue said, "The man that hired us will understand. All we need to do is return the money he advanced us."

The cleric said, "Spent it."

The wizard said, "Same here."

The rogue said, "Fools! I was waiting until we reached the city. Proper supplies will be easier to obtain there."

The fighter said, "We should have hired that ranger."

Almost all of them voiced the same. What a pathetic lot this was. Two days in and already giving up all hope. I once had a woman come through and not give up for a week. I had to secretly protect her by going up ahead of her and chasing away the predators and the fairies and warning off the dryad, but I was having fun telling all the forest creatures just how stupid that woman was. She was lost and going around in circles and did not even notice she had passed the same place six times. I nearly died laughing over that one, and the old dire bear and I still have a laugh over it once in a while. He still thinks he should have eaten her. "Rid the world of the fool human before she causes damage."

This party was really bad, though. I rode up to within a hundred feet of their camp and sat there watching and listening to them, and they didn't even notice. Personally, I could have heard myself coming from a league away. The fire they started was out in minutes, and no one wanted to go for more firewood, as the last one to do so got lost and had to call out several times to find the camp and still would have missed it if I hadn't made a few bear calls myself and chased him in the right direction.

I touched Tom's shoulder, and he quietly started forward. I was actually in the camp before they realized I was there. They scrambled, grabbing swords and armor that they had carelessly set aside. I said, "Nice night. Let me make a few suggestions. Get that fire going and keep your swords close. There are several large predators close by. And store your food up high so they don't get tempted to steal it." I turned to go but stopped. "Oh, and keep it down. I heard you all the way over in my camp."

As I was leaving, they all yelled at me, but the fighter was the loudest. "Sir, we are lost and in need of help."

I turned around. "I am on my way to another job. I have no time to show you the way. Best I can do for you is to point you in the right direction. Where are you headed?"

"The city."

I looked at him for a second and then said, "You can't get there from here. The way to town is that direction." I pointed.

The fighter jumped in front of Tom, and Tom looked at him in a way that would change the mind of a hungry dragon. The fighter moved away but continued. "Didn't you say, in the tavern, that you could lead a group through these woods and get them to the city in record time?"

"Yes."

"Then why can't you lead us there? Were you being less than honest?"

I studied him for a second and then smiled. "I see. When I said, 'You can't get there from here,' I did not mean *I* could not."

The fighter said, "Why can we not?"

I said, "Very well. I will give you directions. Please take this down."

The wizard pulled out a piece of parchment, an inkwell, and a feather pen. "Go ahead."

"Head west toward Lone Man's Peak. That's the peak with the single point facing east and a rock on top that looks like a hat. Take the deer path going toward Lake Shinning. You can tell you're on the correct path by the yellow flowers. Do not mistake them for the yellow weeds or you're lost. Now turn due north, toward the swamp. Don't deviate or you're in elvin territory and dead. At the first sign of swamp, turn left toward the green fairies' lands. The fairies will use spells on you, so prepare yourself. If you don't have passage paid for, then prepare for battle with the lizard folk. At the eastern edge of the swamp, turn off to the south, toward the two witches' lair. Don't go past the fallen juniper log, or you will incur the witch's wrath. There are a lot of fallen logs, but this is the only juniper that is exactly three hands in width. Go north at the log and keep that bearing for three hours or so. Camp that night way back from the Valley of Crying Fog. Don't go into the fog at night no matter what you hear. In the morning, you have about one hour to find your way through the thick fog to the pass on the other side before the day creatures come out feeding. Get all that?"

"I got it, but I must say I don't understand it."

I said, "I am sure you will figure that out, because that is only the first day. The next day is far more dangerous and much harder. Ready to take it down?"

The fighter looked shocked and said, "Any chance we could talk you into leading us through to the city?"

I said, thoughtfully, "I already have a job. All I have to do is show up. However, I didn't actually tell him I would show. It's a dirty job, but it pays well."

"How much does it pay?"

"One hundred gold a day."

He cringed. "I will pay you a hundred and fifty a day to take us through."

I looked at him hard. "You have that kind of gold?"

"Our rogue does."

I asked the rogue, "Are you willing to part with it in advance?"

The rogue sent a hateful look at the fighter. "I am not! However, I don't see that I have any choice. We are lost, and we will lose our job if we are not in the city in two weeks."

I said, "Pay me in advance, and I will have you safely in the city in one week."

He took several platinum bars and a lot of gold from his haversack and handed it over. I had counted it when he took it out and recounted it when I received it. "Very well, I will take you to the city. Pack your things and come to my camp. There is water and a fire with plenty of wood and a small deer on the turnspit."

They scrambled, grabbing everything and tying it to their horses. I checked the camp to ensure they had left nothing behind and found a small bag. "Whose bag is this?"

The wizard came up to me. "My bag of spell components. It is irreplaceable."

I smiled down at him from the back of Tom as I handed him

his bag. I said, "Don't worry, sir. I will take very good care of you for the next week."

He smiled and said, "Thanks."

We camped that night without issue. The next day I took them on the path I had them write down. The wizard tried at first to write down directions in his own words but gave up after several hours. He was totally lost even with directions. I showed them Lone Man's Peak, Lake Shinning, the yellow flowers and the yellow weeds, and the swamp. They saw the elves with their bows only when I made a sign asking them to show themselves. They were startled when eighty elves stepped out from behind trees and they hadn't seen even one. The lead scout came to me, and we talked for a few minutes in elvin. They saw the fairies and the lizard folk, and I talked to both and paid the lizard folk their fee. I pointed out the direction of the witches' lair and made a point of going the other direction at the fallen juniper log. We made camp about a hundred paces from the valley of crying fog.

The sound of women and children crying for help kept them up all night, and several times they wanted to go in and save the poor child or woman. I said, "Go ahead if you want, but that's no child or woman. It is a dryad trying to lure you into her tree so that she can use you for fertilizer."

In the morning, exactly at sunup, I tied all the horses together and tied the people into their saddles. The wizard asked, "Is this really necessary?"

I said, "I'll make you a bet. If, when we reach the other side, you still think it was not necessary, I will pay you one hundred gold. However, if you agree it was necessary, you pay me one hundred gold. Deal?"

He smiled. "You have a deal, sir."

Once everyone was tied together, I picked up a large rotten log and placed it across my saddle. Then I climbed up. I patted Tom and quietly asked, "Ready, Tom?"

He nodded his large head and took off like an arrow. He wasn't fast, but he knew the path better than any creature alive. As we recklessly charged through fog so thick you could not see the horse you were sitting on, dryads came at us. They grabbed at us, trying to pull us from the saddles. I dropped the log, and they attacked the log instead. We reached the end and came out of the fog and onto a cliff that turned sharply west and over the mountains. We were in the pass.

I stopped the horses and untied everyone. I had to help two of the people back into their saddles before untying them. The wizard and the fighter would have been pulled out of their saddles if not for being tied in.

The fighter asked, "What did they want? Why go after the rotten log?"

I frowned. "Cleric! This fighter needs attention, and so does the wizard. Check all others, including horses, for any tiny scratch and heal it, no matter how small. The fangs and claws of the dryads will start a rot that will quickly spread if not stopped immediately. What they were attacking for was food. They'll eat anything rotten, including old logs."

The cleric started healing and performed healing even on those who did not seem to need it, "Just in case." He even healed me. The wizard came over and handed me one hundred gold without saying a word. The fighter said, "The forest is far more dangerous than I thought."

I said, "Wait until later. It gets worse. Much worse."

"Is there any way around the 'worse'?"

I thought for a minute and then said, "One way, but it adds an extra day onto the travel, and I thought you were in a hurry. If you are willing to take an extra day, I will give it to you for free. The savings cost in consumables, including healing potions, will more than make up for my cost of another day."

The wizard said, "We'll take the extra day!"

The cleric and rogue said the same. The fighter said, "I guess we'll take another day. Thank you for getting us past those monsters safely."

I looked at him with a frown. "Good sir, those were not monsters. They are just nature's creatures doing what they need to survive. If you want to see monsters, let's not add the extra day. I assure you we will see plenty of monsters, feel their talons, and fight constantly for our lives."

The fighter actually turned white as the blood drained from his face. He said with a small stutter, "The extra day sounds good to me."

At that point, I took them along the tame route. We had no real encounters. We saw plenty of bears, deer, and moose, one lone cabberat, and other wild things. I had to explain to them what they were and what they did. Pixies, fairies, morning waps, and wolves were our constant partners, though they stayed out of bowshot. This party was so noisy, most of the creatures we saw were only there out of curiosity. They wanted to see what was making so much ruckus.

Exactly one week and one day later, we exited the forest and found ourselves in sight of the city. We came to the city gates, and as we entered, my next job saw me. The old man came up and said, "You're late, but still, I was hoping you would show. Are you ready to take us to Four Corners, or do you need preparation?"

I smiled brightly at him and said, "We can leave as soon as you are ready, sir."

The fighter asked, "You were going to the city anyway. You could have taken us for free."

I turned to him and said, "The route I was going to take would have gotten me to the city in five days. If you think the one-week route was dangerous, then think again. You would not have survived the fastest route, unless you can sneak by an old red dragon and your horses are like my Tom. He can't smell, so dragon fear does not affect him."

The fighter said, "Thank you for getting us to the city. It was well worth the price."

They left arguing with each other over this and that. The old man asked, "You can get my daughters and me to Four Corners faster?"

I said, "Not alive. The two-week route is best for women used to city life. I see you are bringing two pack mules loaded with supplies and a cook?"

The old man said, "Our agreement was you would supply the meat and we the cooking. Besides, my daughters do not know how to cook. They are court ladies."

I marveled at that. "Imagine, a woman that can't cook. Who would marry her?" We left for the simple route, full of butterflies and waterfalls and almost no dangers. At least, I would ensure they did not see the dangers. After all, that's my job.

# The Sage/Sorcerer

The tower was finally finished, and I could actually relax and do a bit of reading. My servant brought me a nice glass of wine from my new wine cellar, the chair I had confiscated during my last excursion looked warm and inviting, and I had a stack of books taken from the library of a lost and long-dead evil wizard. I was all set to relax when someone irritatingly knocked on my door. Bob, my servant, looked at me in exasperation and magically traveled to the front foyer to answer it.

Bob asked, "May I help you, my lady?"

A high-pitched, panicked woman's voice begged, "Please, I need to talk to the sage, and I can't be seen."

Bob said, "Please enter." She came in, and the door shut. "He is in; however, he is not receiving visitors at this time."

"Tell him it is of utmost importance."

"May I ask to whom I am speaking?"

"I am the Lady Roxanne."

"Come this way, please." He led her into the waiting room and asked, "Refreshments?"

"No. Please hurry."

He came up the five flights of stairs and said, "I am sorry, my lord, but there is a rather frantic person claiming that she is the Lady Roxanne sitting in the waiting room. She says that she needs to see you and it is of utmost importance. What would you have me do?"

I put the book down that I had just picked up and stood. "I will see the lady. She comes from a very wealthy family and can pay handsomely." In actuality, her husband of an arranged marriage was cheating on her, and the young lady appeared to be pregnant. Normally this would be no problem, but the young lady was the daughter of the Duke of Kayfire, Duke Edward—a very powerful man that thought his daughter was a virgin and would probably kill any man that laid a hand on her. That the two thought they were in love made no difference.

I took the stairs slowly. It is bad business to allow aristocrats the thought that a sage will come to their beck and call. I normally would not, except in this situation it was most prudent and profitable to at least hear the lady out. I walked silently into the room and stood there watching her cry. "May I be of assistance, Lady Roxanne?"

She quickly looked up and said, "I need advice. My husband is dead at the hands of the duke, and the duke is looking at ruining our family. What can I do to stop the duke, or at least pacify him?"

I stood there in thought. This was not what I had been expecting. So the duke had found out and killed her husband a little earlier than I thought. "Lady Roxanne, did the duke happen to kill his daughter also?"

"I am told that he will be taking her to a cleric in Sea Side City to have the unborn child removed and destroyed. His daughter is distraught, as she truly loved my husband."

"I see." Actually I did not see, but I could guess. She knew about the cheating and approved, and that would mean that, as planned, she was cheating herself. "Have you talked this over with your lover?"

Her eyes told me before she said a thing, "How did you know that I have been seeing Baron Martin?"

I said, "I know more than you would think." Actually, this was good news, as the baroness was paying me handsomely for information on whom her husband was seeing.

"Yes, sage. I asked him what I should do. He told me to pack up and flee. We cannot do that. All our power is here. All our money is tied up. We would be on the streets in months as beggars. I come to you in the hopes that you can find another way."

"There is a way."

"What?"

"I will need time and money to investigate this and determine the correct course of action to ensure you come out ahead in this fiasco. If done properly, your family's standing in the duke's eyes may become even higher than it was before he found out."

Hope and a little greed shone brightly in her eyes. "Higher, how is that possible?"

I smiled. "If I told you that, then what would I have to sell?"

She thought for a moment. "We do not have time, sage."

"I can get you the time. That is not a problem, though it is another expense."

"How much will this cost?"

I acted like I was thinking about this out loud. "Getting the time to pull this off will cost me ten thousand gold up front. The research will include some bribes of very high-ranking court officials, so that is another ten thousand gold up front. After the research, pulling this off will cost approximately twenty thousand gold, and making your family look good in the process and become worth more will cost another twenty thousand gold."

Her shocked intake of breath was expected. "Sixty thousand gold." Tears flowed down her cheeks, but tears don't affect me.

I said, "Sixty thousand gold should do it. My fee for all this will be moderate. I will charge you only five thousand gold."

She looked at me in shock.

I said, "That's sixty-five thousand gold up front."

She exclaimed, "Where will I come up with sixty-five thousand gold?"

I said, "Another request? This one I can answer for free. Your father has a book worth the entire price. A book that he keeps locked up and allows no one to read. I will gladly do all we talked about for that book. However, the book must be given legally. I am not a thief and do not accept stolen goods."

She asked, "You want the *Book of Abominable Gloom*? You are a wizard; it will steal your soul."

I said, "It is knowledge. I would set protections and read it so that I know what it says and why it should never be used. Then, I think I will destroy it."

She stood up in anger. "That book cannot be destroyed. No one knows how. If my father knew how, he would destroy it himself."

"I do."

She looked at me long and hard. "How much for that information?"

I said, surprised, "Are you forgetting your family? You have a very bad problem to work out. Still, the price for the knowledge to destroy the book after I have read it is one hundred and fifty thousand gold. The price for the information without allowing me to read it is one million gold."

She exclaimed, "The king himself could not afford one million gold!"

I said, in perfect calm, "I want to read it very badly. There are some bits of knowledge I need to fill in, and I believe the information is in that book."

She turned and walked to the door, but before leaving, she turned and said, "I will contact my father and see what he says."

"I will be right here. Do not wait long. I can assure you that the duke is not waiting."

She departed, and I sent a telepathic message to the duke's wizard: "Hold off the attack, and be ready for payment."

The answer came back: "Will do. The duke and I eagerly await your next message."

I went upstairs, sat in the chair, and started reading the book I had been reading before. Only an hour later, there was a knock on the door.

Bob instantly answered and let in several people. Bob said, "Please, for your safety remain in the waiting room, and I will see if the sage will speak with you."

He came to me and said, "She is back, and she has her father with her as you said she would."

"Is he carrying anything?"

Bob looked surprised. "Yes, a small chest."

I said, "Then all is going as planned." I stood up and headed downstairs. I stopped at the second floor and listened to the conversation.

"Are you sure this sage can destroy the book?"

Lady Roxanne said, "He claims that he can, and everyone says he is very honest and very powerful. He has high-level connections even in the royal courts. I think he knew about our plight before we did."

"I cannot allow this book to fall into the wrong hands. Our family has protected it for ten generations. Though it has been tempting at times, we have never opened it. To just give it to this sage as payment to get us out of our current dilemma is asking more than my heart can stand."

I came down the last stair and stood in the doorway. "You have the book?"

Her father said, "I have it."

I put out a hand. "May I?"

He put the chest down and used a key to open one side and then opened the other instead. The chest was elaborately trapped. Inside was the book.

I picked it up and set it on the table. I mumbled several spells and then opened it. They all flinched. I said, "The spells I placed on it will keep it from harming anyone."

The old man said, "I did not know that was possible."

I said as I started reading, "There is much you do not know." I only scanned the book, and because of the spells I had cast before opening it, I was well protected.

The old man said worriedly, "What is wrong? Are you all right?"

I said in mock anger, "No, I am not all right, sir. I just wasted sixty-five thousand gold on a book that had nothing in it that I did not already know!" A total lie, but he did not know that. I continued. "It was the same with the *Book of Countless Good*. I paid fifty thousand gold for that book and not one speck of good that I did not already know was enclosed. It is getting harder and harder to find something to learn."

The old man said, "And what will you do with this book?"

I said, "I kept the *Book of Countless Good*, but this book would be a disaster if some beginning mage was to get his hands on it." I took the book and walked outside. "Are your men any good at filling in holes?"

"Yes."

I said, "Good. I destroy this book and your men will fill in the hole. Agreed?"

"Of course."

I set the book down on the ground and pulled out some powder. I sprinkled the powder over the book and it caught on fire—a magical fire that quickly climbed to twenty feet and consumed everything. We could clearly see the book being destroyed. There were several explosions, and then the book lay in dust at the bottom of a thirty-foot hole. The fire was so hot that it cut into the ground, crystallizing the sandstone to glass. "Done."

The old man stood looking at the hole. "Done? When will we be attacked by the god that made it?"

I looked at him with an incredulous look of puzzlement. "We will not be attacked. The powder I used is heavenly, and the book was destroyed as if it were done in Caelum, the planes of the gods of good. We are not at risk."

He actually hugged me. "Thank you."

"You're welcome. Now I need to fulfill my side of the contract. Leave and go about your business and be assured that I will take care of everything."

The old man asked, "Can you truly do this? Can you save my family?"

"If you will leave so that I can get things rolling, then yes. However, I must hurry."

They departed, except a few men to fill in the hole. I went inside, changed clothes for court use, and headed out. The men would surely report that I was in my finer clothes and headed toward the castle with all due haste.

When I reached the castle, I was escorted directly to the king's private chambers and into a small meeting room. There sat the duke, his daughter, the baron and his wife, and the king. I went to one knee and waited.

The king instantly said, "Rise, my friend. Did I not tell you that you never need bend a knee to anyone?"

I smiled at my king and ex–adventuring partner and said the same thing I always say when we meet: "One needs show proper respect in front of others, Majesty."

He smiled with the familiarity. "Sit, good sage. I hear you were successful?"

I took the indicated seat and said, "First, some unfinished business, Majesty." I turned to the baroness and said, "You owe me five thousand gold."

She looked sad and reluctant but took off her ring and handed it over. The baron had given it to her on her twenty-fifth birthday. She said, "This is worth ten thousand and far more to me. What is the answer to my question?"

I said, "You will hear it in my report to the king. I will keep this ring for a while in the hopes that the baron will buy it back—for a slight profit, of course." I turned to the duke in expectation.

The duke motioned for a servant to come forth. The servant placed the equivalent of 250,000 gold in small gems in five bags on the table at my position. The duke said, "My men and wizard verified that the book is destroyed. You read it but gained nothing from the reading. Here is your payment."

I pushed one of the bags back. "I would ask a favor, my duke."

His eyes smiled, but his face turned to stone. "And what would part you from fifty thousand in gems, sage?"

"That you reassure the Lady Roxanne and her family that they are not targets and are looked at in good ways by the Crown. After all, they were not using the book, as someone suggested. They wanted it destroyed as much as you did. They are very loyal."

He motioned for the servant to take the bag and said, "It shall be done. They are innocent of all wrongdoing and seem to have this kingdom's best interest at heart."

The king added, "I will also let them know we are pleased." I looked at the bags reluctantly, and the king said with a chuckle, "And I will do it for free, my old friend."

I turned all attention to the king. "Majesty, you requested that I fix two issues in this kingdom. First, the issue of the book. Second, the issue with the baroness being barren—unable to have children and yet craving them." The baroness took in a breath and waited dearly on my next words. "I have done both, in a fashion." I pushed one of the bags over to the duke's daughter. "Sire, I paid the duke's daughter to seduce the husband of Roxanne so that I could make the duke mad enough to kill him." I pulled out a potion and handed it to his daughter. "Take this. Drink every drop. It will counteract the pregnancy potion I gave you so you will no longer seem pregnant."

The princess said, "Thank the gods. Morning sickness does not a happy princess make."

The duke looked shocked and said, in a tone of disbelief, "You weren't pregnant? I killed an innocent man!?"

I said, "No. I paid her to go only so far. She is good at teasing and then denying. Still, a little longer and he may have become very desperate. You did not kill an innocent man. He was the one using the book." Shock reverberated around the room. I continued. "The others did not know, and I did not tell them, so only the ones in this room know. With his death came the release of over twenty people he was controlling using spells from that book. My duke, you killed a very evil man that was a major threat to this kingdom and the Crown, though you did so for the wrong reasons. You are a very good man, and without proof, you would have never even accused him. The king and you wanted it stopped, and I caused you to stop it. I am sorry for manipulating you so, but it was the only way. Your daughter did great in keeping him too busy to see my plan."

The baroness asked, "And my answer?"

I said, "I apologize again for the deception, but it was needed. I told your husband to pay attention to Lady Roxanne. Having such a handsome man seduce her made her cheat on her husband and gave her husband the time to spend with the duke's daughter. In addition, I added a potion to her drink at the last party that specifically made her pay attention back." I shook my head. "You have no idea what I had to go through to get your husband to cheat on you. I had to have the king order it in person! He would not even take a signed letter with the king's signet. He nearly cut my head off the first time I requested it. If I were not so quick, I would be dead and this kingdom would be in deep trouble. Your husband loves you more than any man I have ever known to love a woman. Books should be written about his love for you. The Lady Roxanne was almost as bad. I had to drug her. Both are totally innocent of any wrongdoing. They were forced on each other."

She took her husband's arm and kissed his face. "Had to be ordered by the king in person. Nearly killed the royal sage for even suggesting it. My, you deserve a reward."

I said, "Not now, later." I leaned in just a little. "Also, I made Roxanne ripe and your husband ready with a little potion I can make. Roxanne is pregnant with the baron's child. She does not know it yet, but it will be evident soon. She will probably seek out a cleric to abort the child. She would never do anything to shame her family or the baron. She happens to love you also, baroness, and it is tearing her apart to think she may do you harm. You want a child? Roxanne is pregnant with your child. She would make a wonderful surrogate mother—strong, intelligent, very lovely. It will tie your two families together and make you both stronger. Especially if you were to go to her and make it known you are not upset but would like her to stay at your home to ensure the child, and she, have no problems. That you want the child and ask her if she would do the honors of creating a little girl for you at a later date."

The baron asked happily, "This one's a boy?"

I knew he would ask that. "Yes. The potion can be made to ensure either, and I figured you would want a son first." I turned back to the baroness. "Knowing your husband is faithful, the woman he was with is also loving of your family and faithful, and that you can have children through her—is that worth the price?"

She laughed. "Very much so."

The baron said, "I will buy back that ring, sage. Give me a few weeks to come up with the gold."

I slid the ring over to him. "You owe me five thousand and five hundred. Just a little profit."

The duke asked, "Where did you get that dust? How did you destroy the book? We thought it impossible. My wizards said the dust you used did destroy the book and that there will be no repercussions. How is this possible?"

I said, with sadness evident in my words, "That dust cost more than I made on this deal. A lot more. Finely ground tears of a good-aligned god are difficult to come by and highly expensive. You do not want to know what I had to do to get them. Suffice it to say, nothing I did will harm this kingdom or any other. It is a cost to me only. One might say that I sold a part of my soul to save my king. The answer would give you nightmares for eternity. Do not ask again."

I looked at the king. "Is destroying the book, killing the source of evil using the book, connecting two great families together, and getting the baroness children—even though someone else—enough to satisfy your orders, my king?"

The king touched my shoulder kindly and with gentleness as he watched my tears. "Yes my friend. You can go back to your books now. And thank you."

"You're welcome, my king." I left, went back to my tower, told the servant I was not to be disturbed, and sat down to read the *Book of Abominable Gloom* in full. The finely ground tears of a good-aligned god were still in the pouch they had come in, as I had used only a small amount mixed with some other ingredients to destroy the fake book. I thought to myself before I started reading, *What people see in good or evil I do not understand. It is all knowledge to me.*

# Country Wizard and Friends

**B**efore I left the university, I bought a pony and pack mule for travel to the big city. I obtained all the food and equipment I would need for camping along the way. I had to camp, as towns and cities are spaced too far apart, are too expensive, and are dangerous. Being in a city without a sponsor is not a good place for a country boy, or a brand-new graduate wizard, to be on his own. The good Father told me, "They'll take you for everything, including your undershirt, if you even look their way, boy."

I know the Father was exaggerating again, but the point was not lost, and Father is a smart man. I originally planned to stay completely away from cities, and I would not be heading to the capital city if not for the job I signed up for.

The sign said, "Beginner wizard needed for housecleaning. We seem to have an infestation of bugarts and pixies. It is beneath the Wizard's Guild of our fine city to help with cleaning pests out of middle-class homes. The work is plentiful, and the pay is good and comes with room and board. Bring friends."

I answered that message and received an affirmation that I was needed and that I should bring friends if I could find them along the way. I did not have any friends that I knew of. Perhaps I would find some. The gods always provide.

Two others left shortly after the new wizard. "Mat, he has to be down this road somewhere. They told us at the gate he left only a few hours before we came by. He is traveling very slowly, so we should be able to catch up quickly."

"I know, Mike, but we cannot run the horses or the mule to death trying to catch him. We could barely afford these old glue-factory rejects. Losing one would slow us down that much more."

Mike looked anxiously up the road while walking his mount. "If anything happens to him, I will never forgive myself."

Mat said, "Me neither. Darn that fool first-year that held us up at graduation. If we could have gotten word to the wizard before he left, we would be on this road together. Now I am worried that bandits or wolves will have his hide before we reach him."

Mike patted his horse. "He needs us, and we need him. Sergeant Lazarus told us 'It's difficult to find a good wizard that you can get along with. If you do, then stick to him like glue. He'll take you far.'"

Mat smiled. "I will never forget the first time we met him."

"Me neither, that was a pleasant surprise. We were practice fighting in the trees near the fence that separates the Wizard University from the Fighter's Guild. He was a first-year, same as us. He noticed that you were limping, Mat, and called you over."

*"Hey! You two. Come over here."*

*Mat and Mike looked up and saw a very young little boy and stopped fighting. They walked over. Mat said, "What you want, kid? Need us to beat up somebody for you? We don't do bully work."*

*"Hi, I'm Doug. I'm learning to be a wizard. No, I don't need you to beat up anyone. I was wondering why you are limping."*

*Mike said, "Busted his leg in yesterday's practice. Here at the fighters' school, people take advantage of your weaknesses. We're fighting two toughs in about an hour, and they paid a couple of the upper class to weaken us up a little. I have a bad arm and can't hold a sword worth spit, and Mat has a sprained ankle and can't move very well. We're* doomed. *This is our final before going into our second year. We fail and it'll be an additional month before we get another chance.*"

Doug looked on in thought. "*I was raised by a cleric of the Traveler. I don't like praying and contemplating anywhere as much as I love studying. People and I don't always get along, mostly because I'm small and weak. There are a lot of bullies in the world. My cleric friend said I should use my magical talent as a wizard. He taught me some minor healing spells to keep me occupied until the university would take me, and I don't think the gods would mind if I used some of that healing on the two of you.*"

Mat asked, "*Really? How much? We don't have but a few coins between us.*"

Doug said, "*Cost? I will consider us even if you do well on your final. I don't like bullies and don't like seeing them get away with cheating. Step closer.*"

Mat nearly stumbled, and that brought him out of his thoughts. "Healed us, then mended our armor. Gods bless him. We pretended to still be hurt for the fight and kicked butt."

Mike added, "That's not the only time he helped us, either. He was almost always out there studying. Dependable, that one. Come on; the horses are rested."

Mat asked as he climbed into the saddle, "You sure we're on the right road? I didn't see any street signs."

"This is the direction the gate guard sent us."

Mat looked worried as he picked up the pace. "I hope the gate guard wasn't messing with us just because we're city boys."

I stopped my slow pace to cool my feet and pick up some free spell ingredients. The horse was not tired, but she was starting to look at the vegetation with a hungry eye. I tied her up where she could feed while I studied some of the local fauna around the stream. There were plenty of weeds and flowers, and I clipped some leaves, seeds, pollen, and flower petals and placed them gently in my spell pouch and then removed my boots and socks, rolled up my pant legs, and waded out into the water. It was getting late, and soon I would need to find a good place to camp for the night. Dinner would be welcome, so I looked around for some fish. Sure enough, trout were abundant, and soon I found a nice, fat one. I used a Telekinesis spell to lift it gently up out of the water, move it through the air, and set it down away from the creek, where it could not flop back in.

I looked at the sky. It would be a wet night, and it was coming on quickly, so I decided to camp up the stream a little. It's not smart to be alone out in the woods and be seeable from the road at night. Still, the woods were sparse at this point and the fire would be within view unless I moved a long way in.

I gathered my dinner, horse, and mule and started walking deeper into the woods. Shortly thereafter, I heard someone yelling my name.

"Doug! Hey Doug!"

I turned and looked. It was those two fighters that were always getting into trouble at the fighters' school. "Hi Mat, Mike, nice to see you. What are you doing out here on the road?"

Mat rode up first and climbed down. He gave me a handshake and slap on the back, saying, "We were looking for you."

Mike added, "As soon as we graduated, we went over to the Wizard University. We heard you graduated, and we wanted to talk. We were hopeful you had a job and might need some protection."

Mat said, "Being out here in the woods alone—very brave, Doug. A tiny guy like you could use some friends that can protect you."

I smiled. "Actually, I do have a position and do need some good fighters. I could use a cleric and rogue also."

They were walking their horses, and when I stopped, they did also. I started removing the tack and saddle from my horse.

Mat asked, "We staying here the night?"

I said, "Yes. It's far enough back from the road that we'll have warning if we are going to have company, our fire will not be easily noticed, and we have cover from the storm."

Mike said, "Storm? What storm?" They were both looking up at the clear blue sky.

I said, "Give it about two, maybe three hours and it will be raining."

Mat asked, "How can you know that? They teach you that at the wizards' school?"

I smiled. "Listen closely."

They paused and listened.

Mike said, "I don't hear anything."

I said, "The bugs are taking cover. Now, look at the birds."

Mat said, "They are all flying west."

I said, "Some are in the trees already, and the others are headed toward their nests to protect their young from the rain. Birds in flight are targets for lightning. Look at the creek. Notice that the water has risen in the last few minutes?"

Mike said, "I'll be a toddler, it has. It's nearly twice the size."

I laughed. "A toddler? The creek is coming out of the mountains from the east. The storm is flooding it. The storm is moving slowly, or we would have heard the thunder before we saw the swell of the creek. This spot is on high ground to protect us from flooding and surrounded by trees to protect us from the wind; and there is plenty of dry firewood, so we can start a fire and have dinner if you two can catch some fish before the storm makes the creek swell too much."

Mat said, "I'll get the fish. Mike, you gather the firewood and start hanging the tarp for a tent. What are you going to do, Doug?"

"I'll start a fire, fill waterskins, and set my own tent. Give me your waterskins."

Mat said, "We can fill skins later. Tents should come first."

I asked, "Have you ever been in the woods during a storm? That creek will soon become muddy and fast. It will be dangerous and far too slippery to fill waterskins in the morning." They handed me the waterskins, and after creating a good tie line to attach my horse and mule to, I headed toward the creek. When I came back, there was lots of firewood, and their horses were also attached to my tie line, making it too tight. I said, "I'm going to loosen the tie line a little. A tie line that is too tight will make it easier for the horses and mule to pull away if they become frightened during the storm. A horse can snap a rope if needed. A loose rope tied to strong saplings so that the entire line gives will make it difficult for the horses to escape but give them room to eat the grass, move out of the way of limbs, and defend themselves from creatures."

Mike dropped off some more firewood and said, "You seem to be at home in the woods."

I said, "Spent all my life traveling through the country from farm to farm. Most nights were spent in a barn or in the woods. I'm an orphan. But I was lucky enough that a cleric of the Traveler, Father Murphy, took me under his wing and took care of me. He's a good man and taught me a lot."

I finished setting my tent and pegging it into the ground, nice and deep. Then I pulled my bow and headed down toward the creek. I pulled out a string and attached it to an arrow. I watched the water for signs of shadows. The fish would be looking for bugs washing down in the swift current. Mat was in my vision to the left, and he was trying to catch fish with a pole and bait. Good luck. I saw a large shadow and cast a Perfect Shot spell and fired. I pulled out five fish that way. I cleaned the fish between attempts. I smiled at Mat while holding up my catch and motioning him to follow.

Mat said, "Nice catch. You're good with that bow."

I said, "Not really. I used a spell called Perfect Shot before each attempt, and I still missed three times. I'm out of spells, except cantrips, for the day, but we won't go hungry. The wind is picking up already, and soon we will have sprinkles. We need to cook the fish before the sky opens up and douses our fire."

Mat said, as he grabbed my arm to keep me from falling down the slope, "Watch your feet, Doug. Thanks for helping with the fish. I don't like going hungry, and they weren't biting."

"Too much food coming down from the mountains. They are not that hungry, Mat."

We reached the top and the fire. I wrapped the fish in gormo leaves, added some bacon and spices, and centered them in the ashes that were starting to accumulate at the bottom of the fire. Shortly we had dinner.

Mat asked, "You only eating one, Doug?"

"A little bread and one fat fish is more than enough for me. I'm small and don't need the energy that two big fighters need."

We talked for a while, and then the storm hit full force. We were in our tents quickly and soon asleep.

In the morning I awoke to the feeling of someone sleeping right next to me. I looked up and saw clothes hanging at the end of the tent, drying. Girl's clothes. I slowly looked over, and right next to me was a very lovely young girl. I whispered, "Thank you, my God."

Her eyes opened just a little. "I am not here for that, little boy. Now go back to sleep."

"It's almost light out. I need to pack up and leave."

She frowned. "Oh darn. Are my clothes dry?"

I touched one and said a simple spell that dried them. "They are now."

She tossed the blanket off and stood up while pulling her undies off the line. "My name is Sara. I am a sister of the Helping Hand. A cleric of Solbelli."

I started pulling on my own clothes and whispered a prayer to the Traveler. "I am called Doug. I am a wizard from the university."

"You worship Commeatus, the god of roads? It is not often you find a wizard that prays to any god other than Magicum, the god of magic."

"I was raised by Father Murphy, a cleric of my god. Sister Sara, what are you doing in my tent? And out on the road during a storm?" We were nearly dressed, so I started rolling up the blankets.

Sara said, "I was traveling to the capital city to visit the temple, and this storm caught me unaware. The stream is covering the road, and I can't cross. The road was so dark I could not see to turn back. I prayed to my god and then let my horse have her way in the direction we were going. She was led by my god to this place. This tent was handy, as the tarp over there had fallen down in the wind and the two under it were holding on to it for dear life. I crawled in, and you never woke. You sleep deeply, quietly, and almost never turn. Those two both snore like dragons and fuss all night. This was the best choice. Did you get your eyeful?"

"I am sorry, Sara. I've never seen an undressed girl before."

She looked at me and smiled. "Don't get any ideas. I needed the dryness of your tent and the warmth of your body. The storm is over, and I can be on my way. Thank you."

I mumbled to my god, "My God, you could have woken me."

Sara asked, "What?"

"Just talking to the Traveler."

"Oh. Do I have time for morning prayers before you take down the tent?"

"If you don't mind my praying and studying while you're busy with your god." I sat down, and so did she. I prayed for several healing spells and then studied my spellbook. When I was done, she also got up. Together we climbed out and started tearing down the tent. I cast a drying cantrip before we rolled it up and then brushed and dried the horses and mules. Sara started a fire and pulled out some black root, bacon, and eggs from her pack. Breakfast smelled very good, and I added bacon and eggs to the pile, saying, "The two fighters will be up soon, and they will be hungry. Their names are Mat, he's the redhead, and Mike, he's the tall one."

"Thanks, I'll get things going. Thank you for drying my horse."

"Not a problem, sister."

"I noticed you prayed for healing spells?"

"Yep."

"You're a wizard; how is it you know healing spells?"

We talked for only a few minutes before Mike and Mat smelled the black root and bacon. All of a sudden the tarp, which was lying flat on the ground with two human-size bumps near the center, raised in one spot like someone had just sat up.

"Mat." The tarp shook. "Mat, wake up."

Complainingly, Mat said, "What?"

"Smell that?"

You could hear someone sniffing, "Black root, and is that bacon?"

I said, "It is almost all gone."

The tarp flew off, and both boys stood up. "Doug! Don't get gree … dy." The looks on their faces were hysterical, as might be expected of two boys in their undies standing there looking at a very lovely girl who was smiling at them as she cooked breakfast. They scrambled for their clothes and hastily donned them. Then they turned back for something to eat. Sara had already put out two plates for them.

Sara broke the silence. "Good morning, boys."

Mat and Mike took the plates and started eating. Mat asked, "Doug, where did you find her?"

Sara's raised her eyebrows at the fighters' lack of reciprocation of her good-morning and the third-party question. "Mat, Mike, this is Sister Sara of the Church of Solbelli. Sister Sara, this is Mike and Mat. They are recent graduates of the fighters' school. Sara, would you please answer their questions? I find it rude to talk about someone when they are right in front of me and capable of talking for themselves."

"I would be delighted. I am a recent graduate of the Church and waiting assignment. I am traveling to the capital city to see the wonderful Temple of Solbelli. I was caught in the storm, and Doug was kind enough to share his tent with me last night."

Both fighters were staring at me while shoveling bacon and eggs into their mouths. I could easily see what their thoughts were, and so could Sister Sara. I decided to put a stop to the issue. "Sara was very quiet. I did not even realize she was there until we woke up this morning. Then it was prayers and starting breakfast. How'd you two sleep last night?"

Mat choked on his eggs. "You slept right through her coming into your tent?"

Sara took offense and said, "Children! Doug, you're traveling with little one-track-minded boys. I needed to get out of the rain. I saw an opportunity with a tent that had actually stayed up in the rain. I did not wake up Doug, as I was afraid for my life. I was lucky; Doug is a gentleman, as I am sure both of you are. Don't feel bad about being a virgin, Doug; they are also."

Mike exclaimed, "I am not!"

Mat said, "Yes you are." They started wrestling in the mud. Sister Sara and I washed the plates and finished packing up. The two fighters stopped fighting long enough to see we were packing, and they started packing themselves.

Mat grumbled. "Their stuff is clean and dry. We and ours are muddy and wet. It will rot before we reach the capital."

Sara walked over and did a cleansing spell on them and their equipment. I followed it up with a drying spell. They both stared at us as if we were demons.

Sara asked, "City boys?"

I said, "Yes, but that is where we are going. I'll teach them the country, and they can teach me the city."

Mat mounted and said, "Be glad to. It's easy. The city is a fun place and a lot safer than being out here in the woods. You don't have to worry about storms, bears, lions, or dragons."

Mike looked around in near panic. "Don't say that. You know they can hear it when you call them. We're not protected in the woods."

I nearly choked. "Mat, my thinking seems to be a little different. Out here I am protected by nature. Bears don't normally bother you if you stand still when you see them and don't threaten them. Act small and insignificant, but be ready to run. They will give chase for a while but tire easily. Don't climb a tree, as they are better climbers than you. Lions normally leave man alone, but if you run across one, just act big and intimidate them. Don't run, as they like to chase down their prey and running will make you look like prey. Dragons do not know when you are talking about dragons. They are very rare and seldom bother humans, especially those traveling in groups. They prefer the bears and lions as food. Some dragons will stop and talk with you, trying to practice the standard language. Still, that is a once-in-a-lifetime experience. In the city, there are diseased rats, rabid dogs, con men and women, and extremely high prices; people lie just for the fun of it and cheat you in any way they can. The guards steal from you, charge you for walking their streets. They toss their waste out the windows and on people walking by, so everyone stinks. The king will have your head for not bowing low enough. The people in charge will kill you just for looking at them wrong. Rich people will run over you if you don't get out of the way of their carriage. You can't trust anyone." I looked at Sister Sara. "Anything I missed?"

She was staring at me, and so were Mat and Mike. Sara said,

"Never been in a city before, have you, Doug? Your viewpoint of a city is worse than their perception of the country."

Mat said, "Diseased rats are in the sewers mostly, and few people ever get bit. We don't have rabid dogs. Vendors will haggle with you over prices and lie about their product, and if you are fool enough to believe them, I would say you might think them con men and women, but the truth is you're inexperienced. People don't lie just for the fun of it. There is always a reason, and yes, if you let them, they will cheat you. The guards are normally good people just like you and me, though some try to make an extra gold or two off country folk. People do toss their waste out the windows, and if you're not ready for it, then it falls on you, but people in the city are so used to it that they never get hit and they don't smell. There are people who come by and pick up the waste to dispose of it at night. The king will not have your head for not bowing low enough. You almost never see the king or any royalty except in parades, and then you are expected to look. A guard may bend you a little lower, but they understand that some just don't know how to show the right respect. The people in charge are fancy and expect you to be looking. They don't kill anyone without good reason, because that removes a taxpayer, and they live off of taxes. It is true that rich people will run over you if you don't get out of the way of their carriage. But they seldom venture out in a hurry and have criers telling everyone to get out of the way, so you have plenty of time. Most city folk will grab you and pull you off to the side if they see you don't understand. If some rich person does run you over, they spend time in front of the magistrate. That will cost them a lot of gold in bribes, and they know that few get rich wasting money. In the city, you don't trust people unless you know them and know them well. What you can trust is that they will do what they need to do to survive."

Sara asked, "I take it you guys are headed to the capital city."

I said, "We have a job there cleaning houses." Her eyebrows rose, so I added, "Of bugarts and pixies. We're looking for people to join us. My contact said, 'Bring friends.'"

Sara said, "Who's your contact, and what is the job paying?"

I started to answer, and Sara smiled. Mike stopped me and said, "Answering that question would be a mistake."

I asked, "Why, Mike?"

"In the city, there are people looking for work. Someone would undercut you, and you'd be stuck in the city without a job."

"Undercut me?"

They all looked exasperated. Mike said, "They would take that information and go to your contact. They would let your contact know that they would do the job for less pay. When you showed up at the contact, they would tell you the job is taken."

I must have looked shocked, as they all laughed. I said, "When we get to the city, I'll keep my mouth shut and you guys lead the way."

Mike looked at Sister Sara and asked, "You looking for work?"

"I could use a little experience. I am a new graduate also."

"Doug, Mat, and I are going to be starting a party of adventurers. We could use a good, reliable cleric."

"Equal shares?"

"Of course, but only after the cost of consumables has been deducted."

They talked for about an hour until all of us agreed on the deal and agreed that we may change it after we had more experience.

We were almost into the forest proper when a man stepped out, blocking our progress. "Halt!"

Mike moved his horse in front of mine. Mat asked, "What's the problem, sir?"

"No problem. There is a road tax for passing into the forest. I am the tax collector."

Mike asked, "You and what army?"

The man smiled in a relaxed way showing complete confidence in his abilities. "I need no army, boy. The tax is one half of all your worth."

Mike and Mat dismounted and drew swords.

The man said, as he drew his own sword, "That's a mistake, boys. I have no problem taking it all off your dead bodies."

Sara said to me, "Be ready for a fight."

I pulled a scroll from the tube attached to my backpack.

Mat said, "Leave now, bandit, and we will let you live."

The bandit said, "Enough talk. Time to die, child."

I opened the scroll, and as they started fighting, I cast a Stay spell. The bandit froze in place. I yelled, "Tie him up quickly; the spell don't last long," and tossed a rope in their direction.

When we had him tied up with fifty feet of rope and every one of us had checked the knots, we started talking about what to do next.

Mat said, "I'm not the kind to kill him while defenseless."

Mike had taken a bad cut and would have bled to death if not for Sara's quick thinking. He said, "Turn your head," and started to draw his sword.

Sara said, "Don't! We can't kill him."

I said, "Mike! Don't you dare cut that silk rope. It cost me five gold. We take him back to town. It's a day out of the way, but it's early, and if we push it, we can be there late tonight. I know the guards. Lieutenant Richard will take him off our hands, and there may be a reward."

Mike turned to look at me. "Reward?"

I did a minor cantrip of Find Magic and studied his belongings. "The dirk and sword are both minor magic. The ring is magical, and the leather armor is magical. The boots he is wearing are magical, so please remove them. In fact, remove all his clothes except his undies. Leave him barefoot and walking. Tie him to the back of a saddle.

We run him into town stripped. His boots, armor, and weapons are magical and now ours. Trade them out for what you have now if you want. Mike, you use a two-handed sword, so the long sword is no use to you; take the dirk. Mat, you use a long sword, so change out. Sara, boots or armor?"

Sara smiled. "Armor, after cleaning the smell off."

"Then the boots are mine. Bandit, choose running alongside or sitting on a mule. Tell us nothing about the magic, and it's running alongside. Tell us all, and it's a ride on the mule."

He tried to haggle, so I said, "It's running, then. Gag him; I don't want to hear his complaining. If he falls, then drag him until he decides to stand up."

My threat worked, and he told us. "The long sword is first level, and so is the dirk. The leather armor is second level. The ring is a ring of essentia, and the boots are boots of stealth."

I put the boots back and picked up the ring. "Anyone want to change out for something else?"

Mike said, "Nope, this works for me."

Mat said, "Me too."

Sara said, "The ring and boots are nice, but the armor is more important to me. If we find a rogue for our group, we can give him the boots for joining. Otherwise, we sell them and split the gold. Agreed?"

We all agreed. We took the bandit back to the town, and as soon as the gate guard saw we had a prisoner, he sent for Lieutenant Richard. The gate guard said, "Hi, Doug, I see those two fighters found you. What you got there?" He looked at the gagged man, who had been trying to get our attention ever since we turned toward this town at the fork. "Well, well. If it isn't the self-proclaimed master thief himself. Mess with the wrong folk, Thomas?"

The thief tried to answer but could not. Lieutenant Richard came around the corner and headed our way. When he reached the gate and saw who we had, his sword came out and he instantly stabbed the bandit right in the gut. Even the gate guard was shocked.

Lieutenant Richard said, "Three times we've had this fool, and three times he has escaped. When he escaped the first time, he killed two of my men. The second time, he nearly killed my daughter, who was bringing him dinner, and he stole my horse. Any one of those things is a death sentence, but this last time he rode the baron's son down in the street. The baron put out an order for his instant death, and this time he won't escape." The lieutenant twisted the long sword, killing the bandit. "No waiting this time. You have been tried and convicted in absentia." He yanked out the sword and cleaned it off on a rag the sergeant handed him.

He looked over at me and said, "Thank you, Doug. This brigand has been pestering our town for years. Every time we capture him, he escapes. These your friends?"

"Hi, Lieutenant Richard, sir. This is Sister Sara of the Church of Pelor, and Mat and Mike are recent graduates from the fighters' school. We are forming a party of adventurers and heading to the capital city. We have a job lined up."

The lieutenant looked at Mat. "Mat, you from the city?"

"Yes, sir."

"Teach this fool wizard to make his answers as short as possible and tell no one your business unless necessary. He is going to be a disaster in the city if you don't school him."

"I'm working on it, sir."

"Good. Where are the bandit's belongings?"

Mat said, "Gone, sir."

"What, you found him nearly naked?"

I started to say something, but Sara placed her hand over my mouth.

Mat said, "No, sir. While he was still alive, he traded his magic belongings for a ride to town instead of a walk."

The lieutenant laughed. "He did, did he? Bet he was thinking of a different town. Well, good for you. Come this way. There is a reward." The lieutenant started back to the office, and we followed.

On the way, Sara motioned for me to keep my mouth shut and removed her hand. I was a little miffed, but I get over indignities quickly. At the office, the lieutenant gave us a note and sealed it. We took it to the money exchanger and received a thousand gold each. We sold what we didn't need and bought a few things we did. It seemed Sara was very good at haggling and very frugal with money. Mike actually had to drag me outside once when I looked too enthusiastic about what I though was a good price. When Sara came out, she was smiling. Apparently she had told the man that if I wanted it, then she did not, and as she turned to leave, he dropped the price.

I said to her, "That's lying."

Sara said, "Something you need to learn. You cannot win if you limit yourself. Open your mind and start using their tactics against them."

That was twenty years ago and the start of my fall into evil. Sara taught me to lie, Mat and Mike taught me to cheat, and the rogue we picked up taught me to backstab. Now I am one of the most powerful mages in the realm. I live and thrive in the capital city, and they love me.

# The Cleric of the Traveler

The sky was a wonderful blue. The storm blew away all the dust and smoke of the wagons and chimneys, making it a nice day for walking the road into the city. There were still puddles that God placed in my way to remind me that life is not a straight road but a series of obstacles we must learn to go around or live with. I choose going around, and others choose living with. I pulled one boy out of a rather deep hole. He never even said thank you. What is the world coming to? No matter. The world is full of good, kind people who are polite. It is our lot to bring the lost sheep back into the flock. I will work on that child if I have a chance.

It always amazes me how little this world seems to be. I have traveled the entire world, and everywhere I go I find someone I have met before. For instance, only one wagon back and coming up quickly was a man I had seen a dozen times. He is always showing up in the most unexpected places. Here in Hempfort, he does not even speak the language, but he was here trying to sell his wares. He would, too. They were good knives that were made of good folded steel. They were not masterwork, though I should be fair and say he was getting very near being a master. They were not magical, but they were strong and flexible, and they held a good edge.

His wagon was just pulling even with me when he yelled out. "Father Dol! Fancy meeting you here. Care for a ride?"

I smiled up at him and answered the same I always answer.

"Though my feet get wet and my shoes wear out, I will walk the path my god has sent me to tread. However, thank you, Mark Knifeman. You are a good man for asking."

He said, "I need to show you something, Father. Please ride, if for just a little."

I could not turn down such an invitation and climbed up.

He handed me a package and said, "Take a look at my latest work."

I took the package and gently unwrapped it. It was the finest blade I think I have ever seen. The craftsmanship was magnificent. It actually had a dragon on the blade with the tail pointing toward the tip. The handle was made of some kind of bone and wrapped in a hide that felt almost sticky. The balance was excellent, and the edge was sharp enough to shave with. The handle was bedded and bellied, the double hollow grind was even and balanced, and the blade had a full tang with a built-in guard and pommel. How he did that, I don't know. The knife handled like part of my hand and felt like air.

While I examined it, he said, "That is the finest dwarven steel I can get. I folded it three hundred times. The edge is hand sharpened, and the full tang was weighted to allow for the weight of the dragon bone and black dragon hide on the handle. It took me three months to make five of these."

I wrapped it back up and said, "Be careful, my friend. To a thief, these are worth stealing. Take them to the Fighters' Guild first and then to the Mages' Guild. Do not show them to anyone else until you have hit each guild. If you are lucky, they will buy them and you will not have any problems with someone trying to cut your throat. Put the money into the Vault Holders' Guild before the day of trading is over. Do not become a target. How much are you asking for one?"

"I am not sure. I would say a hundred gold."

I nearly choked. "They are worth three hundred gold each. Do not sell yourself short. These are masterwork daggers." I pulled out a purse and took out thirty platinum. "I will take that one you just showed me."

His look was one of pure shock, but that did not keep him from taking my gold and handing me the knife. "Thank you."

I answered, "No, thank you, Master Mark Knifeman. You are truly a master now. These are your best works. Say hello to your wife and children when you see them next." I climbed down and restarted my little walk.

He looked back only once and waved. I returned the wave but stepped in a puddle for my trouble. I thought to myself, *Later I will do the spells and add the ingredients to make this dagger magical and holy. It would have been better if I had been there for the making, but we work with what God gives us.*

I took my time and checked out many a traveler. We discussed their gods and mine, as well as the best places in the city for food, baths, and discussions. We also talked about places of interest and places to stay away from, where I could buy and sell items and get an honest price, and what the local issues were. I had studied the area before traveling there and talked to several of my brothers that had walked this road and planted the seeds of our god.

I am here, as always, to plant or water those seeds. Still, it is always best to ask the locals for details before entering a city. When I was young I entered a place called Omar Township. I did not know that all there worship an evil god. It was an interesting experience being arrested and beaten for entering their city and trying to spread the words of my god. I would not change my points of view, so they eventually tossed me out—without my weapons or money pouch, of course. Ah, the wonderful god of travel is always finding ways to teach us the truth. It is our job to learn and remember, and if we don't, then the lesson often gets repeated with increased intensity. Commeatus, blessed be his name, will get it through our thick skulls one way or another.

The gates to the city were open and free for entrance this day. It was the first day of the spring festival often known by the older races as the Time of Renewal. Though people through all the kingdoms celebrate the first day of spring, they all do it in their own way. Here in this country they have a five-day time of "no tax" buying and spending, trading and giving. It is very generous of the crown to allow this and it is a very popular five days. Still, I am told that the crown makes it up from the amount of influx of people spending money in their capital city. That money will eventually change hands during the rest of the year several times and they will make ten times as much taxes as those that party only.

I came to see this wonderful festival for many reasons. First, and most important, I came because my god told me to. In addition, they have several parades and parties that anyone can come to and many that need an invitation. I am also told that they have near-giveaway auctions where they sell nearly everything. At first that bothered me, as they also have a slave auction, but then I found out that the slavery is in good fun and only for a day. Even the prince is sold off as a slave on occasion. The money all goes to the local churches, which is wonderful for the populace. Our denomination does not have a temple at this city and probably will not have for many years to come. We do have a small wooden shrine that we keep up. The Traveler does not care for big, expensive shrines. He would rather have big expensive roads and people praying to him for a good, safe journey.

I never pray for safety unless I am protecting others. I want the experiences. The gate guard motioned for me to come over to the table. Normally, the gate guards of a city have a check point at the gate with a table to place your belongings on while being asked to pay a toll tax for any weapons you are carrying or for finding out your business. This day, everyone was going through without cost or hindrance except those that the guard thinks suspicious. I happen to have one of those faces that screams "dangerous." A child once told me that I look like a bad person. His mother added, "The kind of person that nightmares are made of." I took it in stride.

The guardsman asked, "Business?" as he wrote something into his ledger.

I answered, "Spreading the words of my god."

He looked up and asked, "Any other business?"

I smiled, because this one had some intelligence. "I plan on taking in the sights, spending time at the parties, eating until my gut is ready to burst, and drinking until I pass out."

It was his turn to smile. "You sound like a cleric of the Traveler. Can you prove it, other than your garb and focus?"

My knife was instantly in my hand, and I cut his arm, leaving just a shallow wound. Then I touched the spot and cast a Minor Cure spell. I asked, "Is that enough, or would you like deeper proof?"

His captain stepped up and said, "Our apologies, Father, but we have had a rash of thieves that dress as priests lately. They sell healing potions to the poor and the middle class and then disappear. The potions are poison. They kill very quickly."

I opened my case and pulled out my wares: six hundred potions of Light Healing, three hundred of Heal Poison, and one hundred potions of Remove Disease.

I said, "You are welcome to test three bottles, one of each, in return for a note showing that my wares are true."

The captain called, "Sergeant Kater! Bring forward Archer Jones."

A sergeant went into the guard house and came out with a sickly boy of about sixteen. I instantly went to his side and helped him over to the table. I looked into his eyes and at his skin. "This boy has been poisoned." The captain picked up a potion from my Heal Poison group and poured it down the boy's throat. It took only a second before the boy started looking much better.

I said, "He has lost a lot of his essence. The poison is gone, but he is still weak. May I do a renewal on him?"

The captain said, "Please do."

I pulled out the components and completed a full renewal. "There. Feeling better, young man?"

"Yes sir, Father sir. I feel much better."

I turned to the captain and said, "That was a nasty poison made to weaken the fortitude of a person. I am surprised he is still alive."

The sergeant said, "He took only one tiny bite to check if everything was all right."

My anger must have shown when I asked, "Have you found these murderers yet?"

The captain said, "Not yet."

I pulled out a wand and said, "Have you tried using one of these?"

The captain was now very curious. "A wand? What good would this wand be?"

I said, "It is a wand of Sense Poison. Any cleric can use it. It will last for as long as the person concentrates on what he is doing, which would be looking for poison. It can see through most small, thin stuff: wooden boxes and barrels, clothes, and small, thin chests. It will not work through walls; but for this gate, it can be very helpful. A good cleric can check everyone coming through instantly as long as you don't distract him. He could point out anyone with poison. Now, please understand, some spices are poisonous, as are some pigments for clothing and paints. You still need to be careful how you handle the situation. Do you have a good cleric handy?"

The captain said, "No, but we can get one." He motioned for a soldier to run fetch a cleric, and one took off at a run. "It will take an hour or so. It would be nice if you could stay and handle the situation until one arrives." The captain also sent out guards to shut all other entrances into or out of the city, including the eyes of the needle, or as some call them, the servants' small doors.

I started putting my wares back in my pack. "I would be happy to help you, Captain, as long as it is for just an hour or so. I fully intend to take in the sights of this wonderful city and the festival. It would be a shame to have to be stuck at the gate for five days."

He chuckled. "I am wondering why your wares include Heal Poison and why you would have a Sense Poison wand?"

I looked at him a little thoughtfully. "Does seem like a coincidence, does it not?"

"Yes, it does."

"I wondered why my god wanted me to make and bring so many poison-related objects myself. Now I know." I pulled out one hundred wands of Sense Poison and set them on the table and then pulled out fifty wands of Counteract Poison and said, "Ask any cleric the cost for making a wand of Sense Poison or Counteract Poison, and he will tell you the cost and the sale price—and they are not cheap. I will give these to your city free, except ten of the Sense Poison and two of the Counteract Poison. You may also have all of the Heal Poison potions except ten. My god would have it no other way."

The captain said, "That will surely make you a very well-loved person in this city. Why keep ten of each?"

"I plan on eating and drinking a lot. Using the wands, I will check everything before eating or drinking, and if I find it poisoned, I will neutralize it before consumption. The potions are for when I make a mistake or if I see someone else that made a mistake."

The captain said, "That makes sense, and I will gladly accept your donation to the well-being of this city."

I asked, "Captain, why is it your local clerics did not offer the same? They must have some stockpiles of the same as I have brought. They are common items."

He said, "They did, but they had less than you do by far, and they used them all up protecting the royal family."

I said, "That does not make sense. A simple spell called Magical Banquet would protect the royal family. What temples do you have here, Captain?"

"Sobelli and Valoris."

"Ah, two good gods and many good clerics I am sure, but possibly not experienced enough to do the stated spells. They will work with me. I can help recharge any wand they have. I can also make many more potions if they can find the ingredients. I will help as much as I can before moving on, but I suggest you find the reason for this attack and cut its head from its shoulders as quickly as possible. And, Captain, I am a little suspicious about the manner in which the clerics have handled this situation. Be cautious, and don't rule out clerical foul play. Clerics have been known to be replaced by imposters in the past, and they have been known to be changed against their will. It happens, Captain, so be very careful."

The items I was keeping went back in my magical packs, and I picked up one of the wands. I said, "I must concentrate, so do not disturb me, but listen closely to what I say."

I activated the wand and scanned the area. I pointed out three places where poison was, and they took care of it. I had them bring one small portion of the poison to my area and tie it in a small sack to the gate where I would see it at all times.

The captain asked, "Why do you want the poison there?"

I said, "Great, I just lost my concentration and will need to use another charge on the wand. The reason is so that I can see that the charge is still working. If it goes out for any reason, then I stop seeing that sack as poison. I personally don't need the extra help, but another cleric of less ability may." I reactivated the wand and sat to watch the crowd. There were many priests that came through. At one point someone dressed as a priest of Ultio came through, and he had several vials of poison, and there was also poison on his knife. They took him away for questioning. A few hours later there was a person dressed as a priest of Sobelli coming through, and he was fine, but the two carrying his belongings had enough poison to destroy the water supply and kill everyone in the city. They put up a fight, and I helped end it. A simple spell put them all to sleep. It also put several others to sleep, but we could always wake them up. First, these three were stripped and then manacled, and then they were taken off for questioning.

I looked at the sky and asked, "Where is that other cleric?"

The captain said, "My apologies, good Father, but they are using your wands to hunt the city. They have already found six assassins and saved many lives. The local Thieves' Guild and the Assassin's Guild are very upset that others are coming into their territory and causing such damage, which includes killing off thieves and assassins. They have found another five that they have killed outright."

I said, "We found two, and the others found eleven. You are at war, Captain, and I wonder how many of these fine people are soldiers of another country."

His eyes went wide, and he looked at all the thousands of people trying to come in and thought about all the thousands that had already come in. "It does seem like we have many more people coming in this year than most. Thousands more." He turned to the sergeant and said, "Warn the castle and send me ten good scouts." He turned to another and said, "Go out there and tell that caravan that we are closing the gate early so that we can find room for all the people. Many will have to camp inside the gates tomorrow, as the inns are full, but for this night they camp outside the gates. We will open again at daybreak. Go!"

The soldier left and quickly returned. The caravan was turning off the road in preparation for spending another night out. There were many grumbles, but the captain did not give way. Another priest came up, and I reactivated the wand. Instantly I knew and said, "Arrest that one."

He tried to flee, but the soldiers were very fast. Bolos flew, tripping his legs and tying his arms. They pulled him in cussing and screaming and took him off to wherever they were doing the questioning.

With the gate closed for the night, I was set free to roam the city. I hadn't taken two steps before several people came up to me. The people of the city were not stupid. They knew something was up, and they had figured it out hours before. These people had a place for me to sleep, eat, drink, and party—all for free. I received invitations to high-level parties that I would never have been invited to before this little issue.

I went with them. It was as good as any other place to start, and they promised the best food and wine in the city. So did three other places. I told them I would check out each place and then wander between them all night, sampling the food and wine. They were all on the same block in the high end of the vendors' section of the city, so that made them very happy.

Within an hour, word that they had protections went around, and the four places were very crowded. Still, there was always room for the cleric of the Traveler. They were right. The food was great, and I had to do several spells to take away my drunkenness so I could continue. The women were nice also. As soon as they found out that clerics of the Traveler are not prudes, they flocked to me. Considering my face, that is a miracle that I will spend days thanking my god for. Still, I used a few spells like Dragon Constitution to keep things going, and a full heal to take away the fatigue. I lasted all night, drank several men under the table, and let several women have their way with me. When the morning sun hit our eyes, I was feeling refreshed and ready to go. All others were dead on their feet. What a night! I decided that I liked this city. War issue or no, this was very friendly.

I took two hours to sleep in the arms of a great woman, which refreshed me completely, and then prayed for spells that would set me up for a war-type situation. I had my magical banquet, and when I started walking down to the main gate to check on things, a guard came running up with a message.

"Father, sir. A message from the captain."

"Go ahead."

"Father Dol, please follow this guard. He will lead you to my position. You were correct. We are being attacked. I hope you have something else in those packs. We are going to need a miracle."

I followed the guard to the captain. He was in the castle with the general and the king. As I came in, I saw the king and gave the proper bow.

The king said, "So, this is the kindhearted priest that actually listens to his god and prepares for issues like ours. Rise, my friend. Rise."

I stood up and said, "Any priest that doesn't listen to his god is no priest. It is our life and reason for being to listen and do as told."

The king looked over at his house cleric and said, "I wish all were so faithful." He put an arm around my shoulders and led me to a table where maps were spread out. "I hope you had a good night, Father. It may be a long day."

"I partied all night, sampled your wine, women, and food until I nearly burst, and I am fully ready for the day. The god of travel does not let his faithful followers flounder when there is work to be done."

"I like your attitude. You told my captain that we may be at war. You were right. The good captain sent out scouts and found an entire encampment south of the city. Nearly eight hundred strong. That would not be a threat if we could be assured that the gates would be closed and stay that way. However, with their people inside the city, the gates are at risk, and they could let those eight hundred in without a fight. We actually have a possibility of losing this war, because we cannot guarantee the gates will remain closed."

I said, "True, if the fight was inside the walls, but they made a big mistake. Let's take the fight to the encampment. Surprise them in their beds tonight. You have war wizards plus an Assassins' Guild?"

The king thought for a second. "I have twenty war wizards, but I don't know about the Assassins' Guild." He looked around until he saw someone I pretended to miss as I walked by him. He was trying so hard to not be seen. I didn't want to ruin it for him. The king said, "Rogue, can we count on this Assassins' Guild to fight for us?"

The rogue said, "Normally no, Majesty. However, they are a little annoyed that someone used poison on them, and they are looking for retribution. They helped comb the city in places where we could not go or did not know about."

Someone else walked out into the open, and he did not bow. Swords were drawn and arrows nocked, but the king held up a hand. "You are from the guild?"

"As the cleric of the Traveler knows, I am the king of assassins. I happen to be in your famed city for the party and because my god told me to be here."

The city king asked, "And, your god would be?"

I smiled. "Good gods, bad gods—who cares at this hour." I walked up to him and put out my hand. "Welcome, Brother."

We could not see anything about his vestige except his eyes, and they had makeup and gave away nothing. He was wrapped from head to toe in light stone colors and light gray. After shaking my hand, he asked, "I received your message. What would you have of us, cleric of the Traveler?"

I said, "Simple. Tonight, in their encampment, kill as many of their clerics and wizards as possible. With their magic users out of the way, the city war wizards can fly in and devastate the rest."

"Time of the attack?"

"First dark."

"Payment?"

I pulled out a bag and handed it over.

He opened it and looked inside. He looked at me and said, "How did you gain this, cleric!? I have been hunting it for several moons. We found the thief that took it, but it appeared that someone had found him before we did." He looked in the bag again. "You are prepared. You just bought the entire Assassins' and Thieves' Guilds. We will attack at first dark and quickly leave. We do not want to be in the way of the war wizards. However"—he looked in the bag again—"we will be in the night, taking out anyone trying to leave."

"Done."

"Done."

He disappeared without spell. He simply disappeared. I saw where he was and what he did, but I doubt anyone else did.

The rogue looked astonished and said, "I wish I could do that."

The king asked, "Cleric, you have this planned out well. If they can take out the magic users, we can and will devastate them—and quickly. What did you pay him?"

"The Heart of the Assassin."

Nearly everyone's mouth opened, yet not a word could be heard. Finally, the king asked, "How is it you came by the fist-sized red diamond?"

I answered knowing full well the king of assassins was still there listening. "I caught the thief that absconded with it from the Assassins' Guild in Stoneforge. I was in the wrong place at the wrong time and witnessed him leaving the guild. He could not afford a witness, and so he attacked. I won, and therefore I won everything on his body. I was a little intoxicated at the time and woke up in my room with the heart in my pocket. I very much wanted to return the gem to the king right then and there, as we had met many times before, but you don't walk into the Assassins' Guild with their heart in hand. So I decided to wait until there came a time when I was able to sell it back. This is a good time, and it gains us an easy victory. With the king of assassins guiding the rest, I can assure you the job will be completed—and fully."

The rogue asked in shock, "Why would you want to give it back? You could have been rich and retired!"

"I am a cleric of the Traveler, and I am blessed of my god. I need only what I can carry, a road to travel, a kindness in my heart, and the goodwill of others. What would I do with treasures besides draw unwanted attention to myself?"

The king said to the rogue, "Not all care about wealth and riches, land, and ownership."

I said, "Oh, I have riches. I have the world to travel, the cities and mountains to see, the richness of the land under my feet, the grandness of the trees over my head, the love of good women when needed, and the blessings of good food and wine. What more does a man need? If I need wealth to do something for my god, then he paves a way for me to gain that wealth. It took two artifacts to gain the gold to buy the ingredients to make all that we made for this trip. I had the help of twenty other clerics of my order, and it is very rare to find twenty-one—if you include me—of my order in one place. The celebrating alone should go down in history. Speaking of celebrating, it's time to get back to the party. I'm missing all the excitement."

The king laughed. "We need a temple to your god. He sounds like a fun one."

I looked at him in thought. "If you are serious, building a temple to my god would be easy. Pave the road into town and widen it. Then dedicate it to Commeatus with a little one-room shrine near the gates and some tiny sleeping rooms in the back. No grand ambiance or expensive structures. A place just big enough for a few weary travelers to rest their feet and get out of the cold for a night. He needs no big temple. He is the god of roads and travel. All roads, paths, mountain passes, and sea lanes belong to him. All roadside inns, convenient roadway resting areas, and eating establishments for the weary traveler are his. He is everywhere and with everyone who takes a step onto or into his domain. When you ride or walk along his roads on a hot day and find an unexpected spring of clear, clean water, then know that my god is with you. When you are hot and a tree provides you with exceptional shade, then know that my god is with you. When you pray at the beginning of a trip for a good, safe passage or when returning, give thanks for making it home alive, then remember—it is Commeatus that makes travel possible and grants safety."

The king's eyebrows were up, as he was not used to receiving sermons. "And what about the times thieves steal our gold or orcs attack our caravans?"

I smiled. "What would life be without challenges? Do you expect the gods to make life completely simple? Some gods place obstacles in front of us in order for us to know the difference between good and evil. Some place obstacles in front of us to help out their worshipers who happen to not like us. Our gods watch over us, but their agenda for our existence may not agree with another god's agenda. However, be happy and praise the great god of travel, for my god has taken great interest in your city."

The king asked, "Why? Why is your god so interested in this city?"

I smiled, as he had just caused me to lengthen my sermon. "Why? Because you have a tradition that causes much travel and that pleases my god. Every year, people come from all over the continent to be part of this festival, to have a grand time, to buy, sell, and trade.

It has made my god very happy, and for that reason he has sent me here. He started me on this path seven years ago. Seven years I have followed my god's words in the faith that he had a plan. I battled undead and demons for one of the artifacts. I nearly died fighting an evil dragon for the other. Throughout the trials he put me through, I grew and learned to make potions and wands. I had no idea why, but it is what he wanted, and so I did it along with twenty other clerics that followed in blind faith. In that same faith, they handed me their wares and blessed my travels to your city. In that same faith, I came with my god's blessings in hand in the form of potions and wands for your protection. It was my god that placed me near the Assassins' Guild on that faithful night so that I would have the payment needed. And now I know why he placed me on this long journey, and I look forward to the next." I smiled. "Hopefully, that will not be until I have sampled some more of your food, wine, and women."

The battle went as planned, and I was invited to the grandest of parties. Don't tell the king, but I took a few of his best bottles of wine for the road, and quite a bit of food. I already knew my next destination, and it would be a long, wonderful journey. Still, my god knew me and told me to start the day after the close of the festivities. You have to love a god that cares so much. I know I do.

# The Wizard: Not What They Seem

"I hate traveling by sea. I would much prefer riding or walking. Why did I allow you to talk me into taking a ship? What was I thinking?"

*You were thinking with your head for only a few seconds. Did it hurt?*

"Not then but it does now."

*That's the cheap wine we drank last night while the sailors took you for the gold you allowed them to see. I told you we needed to stop drinking.*

"True, but if I listened to you about everything, we would be penniless farmers by now."

*Farmers, fletchers, any trade not associated with adventuring. I don't want to die, and I am sure you got us into something this time that is going to kill us off, and quickly.*

"Oh, be quiet. Another is coming."

I looked over to the left and watched her saunter across the deck. Though the ship was swaying and heaving, she walked with such grace that you could not tell there was movement unless you dragged your eyes off the wench. She says she is a lady, but I have seen otherwise and sampled the otherwise myself. She is no lady. Still, she has the sailors baffled, and that got us passage. *Darn, she saw me. Here she comes.*

*I told you she was bad news.*

"Quiet, you little pest!"

She walked up, and in a voice like cream pouring over iced cake, she asked, "Talking to your familiar again, wizard?"

"The name is Dan, and yes, I was." It did not help that she thought me insane for talking to a lizard.

*Lizard? Lizard! I will have you know I am a descendent of the great worms. I have dragon blood in me just the same as you do. Don't call me a lizard.*

"I was thinking about what she thinks, not what I think. You are far too touchy."

*Touchy? Touchy! I'll have you know t—*

I stuffed him into my side pouch and drew the string tight. Talking with the "lady" left no room for distractions if I wanted to keep my wits and possibly my skin.

I said, "It's another nice day, Lady Scott. The captain tells me we are making record speeds and should pull into land three days ahead of schedule." I looked her up and down, trying to keep the distaste out of my expression. "You seem to be faring well. Was it two or three sailors last night?"

She looked back and said, "Three. I am a little concerned, Dan. Are you helping us along? The wind seems to always blow in the best direction and always just enough to give speed and not tip the ship. That is very unnatural for this time of year."

I asked, "Would you rather have the storm that I am manipulating, or the manipulation?"

"Storm?"

*Rogues. Self-centered fools*, I thought. Out loud I said, "We are in the eye of a typhoon at this time. I am on deck to ensure the typhoon understands to leave this tiny ship alone. Sadly, it is very mad and will probably destroy this ship the next time it finds it."

"Sure. You think I believe any of that rubbish? You are here trying to get some fresh air after drinking and playing dice all night long. How much did you lose?"

"Why are you interested?"

Quietly she said, "You carry our treasure, and I will not have you gambling it away."

I said, "Fool child. I gambled to learn the mood of the sailors and ease their concerns about the others. It was only a hundred gold, which was just enough to make them happy but not enough to make them suspicious. I kept my wits and ensured they knew you were a lady but a very loose one. I also gained valuable information about our next port. We leave the ship there. Please tell the others."

She started to turn while saying, "A typhoon doesn't have a mind. You can't talk to a stupid storm."

As she crossed the deck, a side wind came up, blowing her dress above her head, knocking her hat into the water, and causing a sail to snap her in the backside good and hard. It took everything I had to keep from laughing. I winked at the gigantic air elemental that was the center of the storm, and he winked back. The "lady" tripped her way back under the deck, nearly falling down the steps.

It wasn't long before the cleric came up looking for me. "Dan, I'm happy to see you this day. My god and I have been talking, and it seems that you have placed this ship in danger by upsetting a typhoon. I am disappointed in you."

I looked over at him, thinking, *Sure, it was your god, if she stood on two legs and had a freshly bruised back end.* I said, "Hello, Nick. Con any sailors into believing in your god over the other gods lately?"

His face darkened with anger for only an instant. "No. They laugh at me, saying that their god is giving them favorable winds and fair seas. I cannot get any of them to listen."

"Whoops."

He looked at me longer and then asked, in a stunned tone, "You are controlling a typhoon, aren't you?"

"Yes. You want to say something about his mentality like the 'lady' did?"

"I saw the lady. I don't think so. Can you get it to leave this ship alone after we depart?"

"Sure, but it will cost me dearly, and I don't think there is anyone on this ship worth the effort."

"What is the cost? I will pay it."

"Your soul."

His chin dropped, so I turned toward him for the first time. "The way you control an ancient air elemental is not by the power of the mind. It is by the power of the sprit. Ask your god if you do not believe me. I am using my sprit to make the air elemental do my bidding. If I did not, this ship would already be broken and sunk. It turns out the elemental was hired to destroy us. I am postponing that destiny in the hope of getting off before I lose control and we all die. If you want to save the ship longer than I have already saved it, then you must use your soul and bind it to this ship for all eternity. It will no longer belong to your god or to you. You will become part of the ship and it a part of you, and when the ship dies, so will your soul."

The cleric stared at me for a good, long time and then smiled as he clapped me on the back good and hard. "That's the most fantastic story I have ever heard. The lady was right. You are a grand liar." He walked away, laughing until the yard arm slammed him in the head. I looked at the air elemental, and he very guiltily shrugged his massive shoulders. I smiled and said in his own language, "They believe so much trash about the gods and so very little about the true world."

"Let me go, and I will teach them a lesson they will not forget."

I laughed loud and hard, startling several sailors. I yelled up into the typhoon, saying, "I will let you go when I am safely on dry land, unless you give me your word you will not attack me again."

"I did not attack you personally. I was ordered to destroy this ship. How was I supposed to know a powerful wizard was on board?"

"Who ordered you to destroy this ship, and why?"

He said, "I will not tell you that."

I said, "I will not let you go." Only the captain understood the language, and he came to me.

"Wizard, you seem to be talking to the wind, and he seems to be talking back."

I thought to myself, *Here it comes.* "Hello, Captain, someone hired a gigantic air elemental to create a typhoon to destroy this ship. As no one except the crew knows my party and I are aboard, I have to believe it was something someone else did to upset a very powerful and very rich person. I am controlling the elemental, and it is costing me dearly. Can you please explain?"

He turned from me in anger and yelled, "Devin!"

A very handsome young man came across the deck with a look of fear. "Yes, Captain."

"You were in a hurry to get away from that last port. I want to know why."

The young man smiled and said, "There was this young girl I found, and we had a good time. At least until her father found out. I was fleeing for my life. The man is very powerful and rich. How was I supposed to know the girl was the local sage's daughter?"

The captain backhanded him so hard he fell nearly over the deck. The air elemental said, "Give him to me and I will leave you alone."

I levitated him up and over the side. "He is all yours."

The typhoon left with the screaming young man, and the weather turned to a calm, peaceful day with nearly glasslike waters.

The captain turned to me. "Shame, he was a good deckhand. Liked the girls a little too much, but a darn good deckhand, and those are hard to find." He turned back to his ship. "Unfurl the sails, set the watch, look for a breeze. Find me some westerly or we are rowing. Move it, you scurvy lot, or your livers will steam on my dinner plate tonight."

I said, "Want a gentle breeze, Captain?"

He said, "Let's try it the natural way for a while."

I laughed silently and went below decks to check on the rest of the party. The fighter followed me down and walked over to a corner.

Why I threw in with this lot is easy to remember. There is a book I want in the treasure they are after. They know the location and I know the book. They want the treasure and I agreed to take my equal portion and any magic books we find as part of that portion. I get the knowledge I want and they get a wizard way past their level of experience. They don't know or understand that yet, so let's keep that a secret. I have them thinking I am a nutcase and apparently a liar. Works for me. I did not lie and I am not insane but I do not care what they think as long as I get that book. I have not determined if I will let them live after I have the book, except the fighter. I may if I think they will be useful at another time. At this time I see no use for them except to guide me to the book.

I stepped into the little cabin where they were gathered talking about how to reach their destination once off the ship.

The ranger, a man called Coreman, was saying, "We can buy horses in the town we are sailing to and then travel up over the mountains to the pass at Wayward Junction. A couple of mules to carry provisions and we should be there in a few weeks."

I interjected. "I can turn us all to vapor, and we could fly above the mountains to our destination."

Laughter filled the room. The "lady" was nearly choking on her drink. The ranger said, "Enough of this foolishness. We need a real plan, not some wizard's dream of grandeur. Now, as I was saying, we have enough to buy anything we may need for the trip. I would suggest some winter clothes, my lady. It will get cold at night in the forest and up over the pass. You will freeze if all you take are the clothes I've seen so far."

The "lady" said, "Well, we wouldn't want that, now would we. Is someone taking notes? This is a good time to determine what we will need, and how much of it."

The cleric said under his breath, "Why? You won't be able to read them." Aloud he said, "Good idea, my lady. Do you happen to have parchment, ink, and a pen?"

I made a tiny gesture, and parchment, ink, and pen were floating in front of me. I said, "Go ahead; I will gladly take notes for you."

They looked at the parchment just floating there and waited for it to drop. It did not, and they looked at me with a little worry. I said, "Handy trick, isn't it?"

The cleric stood up and looked all around it. "Yes. Is this spell divine, arcane, or either?"

"Arcane."

He said, "Oh darn. I can't do arcane."

I said, "If you could, I would be pleasantly surprised."

The pen was posed over the paper, and the ink was drying out, so I said, "Pen, this will be a list with amounts. We will need five horses with tack, and two of those will be sidesaddle."

The fighter interjected, saying, "I don't ride sidesaddle."

I looked at her. "Oh, I forgot. You know, sometimes I see you as more of a lady than the pretend one." She smiled. The pretend one did not.

"Pretend!"

She started to throw something at me, but the ranger stood up and said, "Stop!"

I said, "Pen, change that to only one sidesaddle. Add in two mules with harness and packs, and winter clothes for all, with warm cloaks. Fur lining for the ladies and heavy for the men. Include supplies for six people for five weeks, three two-man tents, cooking supplies, and waterskins. End pen." I thought for a second and asked, "Ranger, what is the terrain like?"

"We can expect deep forest for the first ten days and then mountains for the last. Why only five horses? There are six of us."

"Coreman, I have my own mount. Now, is there plenty of drinkable water without spending time looking?"

Coreman thought for a second, laughed, and said, "I did not see you pack a horse, wizard. Is it in your pocket? As for water, not once we reach the mountains. There will be a lack of streams up that high."

I ignored the ranger's remarks and asked, "Good Cleric Nick, can you create food and water?"

Nick said, "Actually, no. I could if we had scrolls, but the spell still eludes me."

I turned to the pen and said, "Pen, of the waterskins, mark them as twelve and place them as two each. Add eight scrolls of Produce Food and Water." I turned to the ranger expectantly.

Coreman looked at the pen and said, "Pen, we will also need thirty magic glow rods." As the pen wrote, the ranger was totally shocked and nearly ready to pull his sword. He calmed down and continued. "We will also need six climbing kits, two hundred feet of knotted rope, a grappling hook, a shovel, and sixty arrows for the ranger." He turned to the rest. "Any consumables you need?"

The lady said, "Pen, add in two lockpicks, twenty arrows, and three bow strings for a composite longbow. I will also require six flasks of acid."

The cleric said, "Pen, I will need five holy waters, twenty bolts for a heavy crossbow, and a flask of oil with rags for keeping my armor rust free."

I said, "Pen, do not add reasons." Everyone watched as the pen moved backward and the ink removed itself from the page. We continued making the list for some time, and the list was long, so I said, "What you ask for you will get, but you will also have to carry it once we can no longer use the horses. Unless you can talk someone else into carrying it."

The lady panicked and said, "Pen, change the amount of acid flasks to two, please."

The ranger asked, "What is the acid for, my lady?"

"Rusted or corroded locks and hinges."

"Will two be enough?"

"Yes, but three would be better."

The ranger said, "Pen, place two acid flasks in my section and one for the lady."

She smiled and said, "Thank you." Then she asked, "Who here cannot climb? We may need block and tackle."

I raised my hand but added, "I can fly, so you will not need to lift me."

The ranger turned to me and said, "I have seen that before, but I would prefer that you save your higher-level spells for fighting. We do not know what denizens may have inhabited the site after this many centuries."

I nearly choked, as if a simple Fly spell was anything near my higher-level spells. I said, "Pen, add some thorn fire salve." To the ranger, I said, "I have a wand of Fly with fifty charges. It's only good for short flights but should get me up a cliff or across a cavern."

The cleric said, "Nice resource. Why the thorn fire salve?"

"Bug repellent."

Everyone said, "Pen, add more thorn fire salve." They looked shocked at each other and burst out laughing.

The pen looked confused, so I said, "Pen, disregard that. Add one flask of thorn fire salve for each person, for a total of six. End pen." I picked the parchment out of the air and handed it to the ranger, our fearless leader.

Coreman took the parchment and read it aloud. "This looks good. If I think of something else, I will ask you to add it, Dan."

I nodded in agreement.

Coreman looked at me and said, "I hear we dock tomorrow."

I pretended to be a little shy about the answer, as if I had made a mistake.

Coreman, Nick, and Lady Scott yelled, "What did you do?"

The fighter, Sepal, said, "Oh, don't blame him. He was fighting the typhoon and bending it to his will when he found out what it was sent after. Apparently a deckhand seduced the daughter of a powerful wizard in our last port of call. The wizard was not happy and sent an air elemental after the ship to destroy the boy. Dan handed the deckhand over to the typhoon, and it left. In doing so, it also took all the weather with it. The captain is looking for a wind but is not finding one, and therefore our sails are slack. Dan offered to create a wind for the captain, but he turned Dan down, preferring a natural wind. They are up there watching for any signs of a breeze. It may be that we will find ourselves stuck on this tub a few days longer."

The lady exclaimed, "You were actually controlling a typhoon!"

I smiled.

The cleric said, "You were not kidding about using your soul, were you?"

I said, "No. I am very tired. Fighting a typhoon is difficult work. I am going to bed for a while. Call me if anything important happens."

I left for the hammocks in the boatswain's locker up front—bad place to be in a storm, but a good place to sleep in a calm. It is very seldom that anyone went there unless the ship needed repair; therefore, I could get some sleep without disturbance.

I must have slept well, as I was awakened by my thorn-dragon familiar named Piper.

*Hey, you wretched primate, get up; we are missing breakfast!*

"Breakfast! Already?"

*Yes, yes. You were very tired after your battle, and you slept eleven hours. I missed dinner. Now get up. I am hungry.*

I rolled out of the hammock. It is amazing how comfortable they are when the ship is gently rocking. Rocking? The captain had found a wind. Good news, that. I gathered my belongings and cast a quick cleansing spell so I did not smell so bad. I studied my spellbook, and then I headed over to the galley.

Upon entering the galley, I found that I was a little early. I looked at my shoulder, where Piper sat, and asked, "I thought you said we would be late?"

Piper looked put out. "Yes, late for the choicest bits of bacon. Smell that. The cook has ham!"

He flew off my shoulder but stopped short of the cook. The last time he tried to steal from the ship's cook, I had to rescue him from a quickly heating covered pot of beef broth. The cook warned me that "He don't have much meat, but what he has is mine if he attempts to steal from me again." I had the cleric heal him before I put him away long enough to get over his trauma.

The cook had actually taken a liking to the pest and started saving choice bits for someone that actually appreciated his cooking. I didn't want to burst his bubble, so I didn't tell him that Piper would eat almost anything, especially if it had been cooked in thick grease.

I took a seat near the starboard porthole. The weather was picking up a little. I could see the small waves bearing white caps, indicating that a good wind was blowing. I closed my eyes and checked for unnatural sources of wind, and there was none. When I opened my eyes, the rest of the party was entering. They all sat around me. They were looking rather uncomfortably at me and being exceptionally quiet.

Piper took that moment to fly past my face and land on the table next to me. The cook had given him a small ham steak, and he was doing his best to tear into it.

Coreman started the questioning. "Dan, it has come to our attention that you are not the wizard we thought you to be. We were supposed to meet a wizard of about our experience whose name we did not know. Controlling a gigantic air elemental, the pen trick, and turning us to mist? These are things that someone of more experience would do. At least, more experience than you told us."

I smiled. "You approached me, remember? No one asked my level of experience. You questioned me on what you needed me to do, and I let you know I can do those things."

The ranger added, "Yes, but you made it seem like it was all you could do. Your look said that it would be taxing but you could squeeze it out if needed."

I smiled. "Squeeze it out. You have a funny notion of magic for a ranger. In addition, you have mistaken my facial expressions as being barely able. In truth, I was thinking that I can revert back to doing tiny, insignificant, little magic if needed, but it would be embarrassing."

The cleric asked a good question. "What is the highest circle of magic you can accomplish?"

I said, "Oh, I suppose I can squeeze out a ninth or two."

They all looked at the cleric, as they had no idea what that meant.

The cleric was staring at me as though I were infected. "Who are you? If you can do ninth-circle spells, then you must have made a name for yourself."

"I am Dan. That would be short for Demos Allen Normon, son of Bathalla Allen Norman, who was the third illegitimate son of Demragonness."

The cleric slowly pulled his morningstar. The ranger, seeing this, went for his weapons. I sat there doing nothing but watching. The cleric asked, "Demragonness? The dragon that leveled Silentia in one day because she was looking for a thief?"

I said, "The same, but would you not be upset if someone absconded with your only egg for the next five hundred years?"

The cleric yelled, "That was not the people's fault! It was a thief!"

I did not lose my control like the inexperienced cleric. I quietly said, "The people allowed the Thieves' Guild to stay and prosper, the city guard did nothing, and the king never took a stand. I suppose no one ever mentioned that my grandmother begged the king and the people for weeks to help her find her egg, and they attacked her."

The cleric calmed down. "That was not part of the story."

I said, "It never is."

The cleric put his morningstar away, and the others sheathed their weapons. I turned a little and said, "Fool woman. You think I did not know you were there?"

She put her knife away and sat down opposite me. "I suppose at your level you would."

The cleric said, "You are a third white dragon." It was not a question, just a statement of his known facts.

I set him on the correct path in his thinking. "I am one-quarter white dragon, one-quarter gold dragon, one-quarter human, and one-quarter unicorn." I looked up with one eyebrow raised. "Don't ask me how that last happened, as I have no idea."

The cleric perked up a little. "Then you are one-half of greater good blood and only one-quarter of evil blood. Does one not war against the other?"

"Constantly, but the unicorn blood always wins out over the rest. In fact, it was a little upset with me giving away that sailor."

The ranger said, in an attempt to justify my continued existence in his own mind, "I have heard that even Caelums considers unicorns pure good."

Piper rolled onto his back and started licking his paws. I scratched him on his full belly, and he stopped. His eyes closed, and he instantly started drifting off to sleep. Then I said, "I fight every day to keep a balance between good and evil. It is difficult to put good in its place and let evil come out more. But I have not given up trying."

They were all looking at me, shocked, until the fighter smiled and said, "He's joking, people."

I smiled back and asked, "How'd you know?"

She looked stern and answered, "You can't lie worth spit. Your entire body gives you away. Though you do try more than you should. Still, with this group you have been very honest. Is that because they didn't believe you anyway?"

"Yes. You have an excellent mind. I would not think anyone would have figured out the things you have. Not at your supposed level."

It was her turn to smile. "Figured that out, did you?"

"It wasn't difficult, Princess Seanna Pallapical. I am surprised the others did not see through your calm demeanor. It is good working with someone of my level again."

"I feel the same. I like knowing that a wizard of your reputation is with us."

"Thank you. I assure you the feeling is mutual."

The princess continued. "Incidentally, going by cloud would be so much better, but I don't think the rest are ready for that. Please let them do their work themselves. Step in if things start getting messy, but let them do their part in this party. They cannot grow if we do not let them."

I said, "Not a problem, Princess, but I will not step in if they do something really stupid. They need to live with their mistakes, even if it means death."

"Good wizard, our ranger seems to be a planner, and that is a good thing. He is not the type to run into traps or ambushes. We will do well."

"I have agreed to follow him, and so I shall, but not to the extent that he obtains an opinion that we will pull him out of any trouble he gets into. I prefer he not get into trouble."

All this time, the rest were going back and forth with their heads as if they were watching an archery tournament. Finally the ranger said, "Stop! Stop, please. Is there anyone else that is not what they seem?" There was no answer, so he asked, "Dan and Princess, why are you in this party? You do not need us."

The princess said, "I'm bored."

I said, "I want a certain book that happens to be where you are going."

The princess said, "And the next one of you who calls me Princess will get a fat lip, including you, Dan. Mind that."

I bowed and said, "As you wish, my lady."

Lady Scott asked, "What do we call you then, Dan?"

I said, "Dan is good for now."

The princess said, "Yes, but when you are in his royal courts, Majesty would be better."

The ranger placed a hand on his forehead and moaned.

# The Fighter

I arose from a good, solid sleep at the slight sound of rustling in the bushes. I stayed perfectly still, waiting, listening, keeping my eyes closed so that they would think me still asleep. He came slowly—oh, so slowly—into the little clearing. My back was turned to him and my hand away from my blade. Slowly he crept. So slowly I almost fell back asleep. That would be a bad mistake. When I felt his breathing and movement above me, I moved. Even though I was going fast, the movements seemed to take forever. His knife was coming down as my fingers wrapped around the handle of my blade. I moved my head just enough to let his blade pass on the right side of my face while mine met ribs and slid through to heart. He crumpled onto the spot where I had been but had moved from.

I took a second to feel my face and hair on the right side. "Good, no blood." His poisoned blade had not cut me. I crouched there waiting, listening, watching for signs of another. They always send one, never two. I heard myself cuss, "Assassins!" and then I spit to clean my mouth of the word. They had found me again. It was time to move.

I donned my armor and set off in a northerly direction. Up to this point, I had stayed away from the north. It was said that demons live in the north.

Somehow, one way or another, I had to stop this madness. The fight had been fair. He had attacked me with blade drawn and eight men helping, and I had killed him bare-handed. It was not my fault he was the son of a rich merchant or that he had a weak neck. How was I supposed to know someone who was trying to kill me was the only son of a shipping tycoon?

I ran through the forest at night using my mind to picture the overgrowth and the path—a trick of magic I learned from the elves. I was fast, but they always managed to find me. I stopped. They would find me again. I was not hard to spot. The description on the last poster said, "Seven feet tall, nearly three feet across the shoulders, can run in full plate while carrying a full load, extraordinarily handsome with chiseled features, all in perfect proportions. Long blond hair (be careful—he could get it cut or grow a beard). He is wanted for murder."

I talked to a local sheriff about the poster and its legality, as I had already been dubbed not guilty by the courts and had the papers to show it.

He told me that as long as the poster said, "Information about where he is only" then it was perfectly legal.

The sheriff suggested my next step. I tried hard to keep this from happening. However, I am not the kind to run and hide for the rest of my life, so it was the only choice I had. I turned and headed west, back to where it had all started, back to the city where this tycoon lived. The only way to stop these assassins was to remove the one paying them. He was rich, powerful, and protected. *First things first,* I thought. *Remove the wealth, power, and protection.*

As a young boy, I had to be very careful and move very slowly so as not to harm another. The ones that did not know me thought me dumb because of my slow speech and movements. The ones that knew me, or had picked on the slow boy, knew better. At the age of ten I was sent to the guild as apprentice to the master swordsmith. I tended the bellows, toted the iron and nickel, and did all the heavy work while learning the craft of making a fine blade. The guild taught me weapons—all weapons. I excelled at bow, blade, and staff until no master in the guild could teach me more. I became the teacher.

I was sent on many a mission, and every one was completed. I helped stop the Blackhearts Band from their thieving ways. It's hard to steal when you are dead. I was with the party that toppled the Tower of Blood and killed the purple wizard. With my hands around his neck, I made his face match his robes before he died. It was I personally that killed the champion of King Richard and ended the six-year war with Trident. And now I was going to kill a certain tycoon. But I wanted to make it fair.

I headed into a printing office in the nearest city. I had them make up the following poster:

Wanted (information only): the whereabouts of Lord Gillion, information on who he sees or sends messages to, his shipping concerns, where his warehouses are, and especially who tells him about me.

A fat little shipping tycoon called Lord Gillion has been sending assassins against me for two years, and I am tired of it. His foolish little son decided he wanted to make a name for himself and tried to kill a hero of the crown. He attacked me with eight of his friends, and I won. Because the son died in the attempt, I was arrested and this issue went to court. The courts proclaimed me innocent of any wrongdoing. "Self-defense." However, the father, Lord Gillion does not agree with the legal courts and seems to be backed in this by someone of high authority. He has to have someone backing him, or he could not continue to find me so easily.

Therefore, I proclaim that Gillion, that high authority, and anyone who turns information about me over to another are trying to kill me. In the name of self-defense, I declare that I am at war with Lord Gillion and his higher authority and that I will hunt down and kill anyone who helps him in any way. I am tired of running from the assassins he sends to kill me. It is time for him and all his enterprises to start running!

Signed this day,

Sir Chris the Demon Slayer, Knight Hero of Formartor, Destroyer of the Brethren of Slaughter, Defender of the High Pass, Hero of The Trident Wars, Crusader of the Last Blessing

I turned to the one taking the note. "How much to put a drawing of Gillion's face on this poster and then post it up next to every poster of me he has put up?"

He thought for a second and said, "As we are the ones he hired to make and post your poster throughout the land, I suppose it will not be difficult to determine the amount of posters needed and where to put them. I would suggest you send one poster to every 'high authority' in the land so that they know you are looking for one of their ilk."

"Good idea."

"You are trying to get people to stop helping Lord Gillion?"

"That is the first step in my plan."

"This is a good way to do so, and it is very legal to openly declare a war against a man you believe is trying to kill you. To war otherwise is illegal. This will ensure that the local constables stay out of your way. By law, they cannot interfere with someone's personal war. However, be warned. Lord Gillion is very wealthy and can now hire mercenaries to hunt you down openly."

I smiled. "How much for the posters and the posting?"

"A thousand gold, Sir Knight."

I opened a small bag of plunder from my last adventure against an evil dragon and pulled out one small gem. I handed it to the man, saying, "That should pay it in full."

He took the gem and checked it out under a lens. His eyes went wide, and he said, "A fire diamond of exquisite beauty. Yes, this will pay for everything." He watched as I made the bag disappear—a trick I learned from a rogue during a long trip. The printer could easily tell that there wasn't much in the bag. I keep the rest of the treasure well hidden. Mostly because I don't like paying taxes.

He said, "Sir Knight, you're going to need a lot more than that little, almost empty, sack if you are going up against Lord Gillion."

I said very nonchalantly, "I am at war with a tycoon. There will be plunder."

His smile increased tenfold. "Send me news as the war progresses. I will print it and sell papers."

I said, "I will try."

He quickly scribed a note, signed it, and handed it to me. "Show this to any of our fine printing offices, and you can give them your news without worry of them telling on you."

"Again, I will try, but I don't want to be known for visiting any one place more than once."

"Understood. Good-bye, Sir Knight, and good luck."

I left and disappeared into the forest. I waited two weeks and then checked in another town to see if my posters were up. One was, and people were standing around talking about it.

A man said, "Gods, a war within our own people."

A woman said, "What's new. We have petty little wars all the time. However, this is the first I have ever seen published."

Another woman said, "I had no idea that the one Lord Gillion wanted information on was one of our own knights, and the hero of the Trident War as well. Gods, I turned in the hero, our savior, the king's friend."

A man said, "We all did. I won't anymore. If he shows up, I

will tell him anything I know about Gillion, and it won't cost him a thing. I never liked that rich bastard, and his son is just the type to try something like that."

A woman said, "I don't trust the courts. They always side with the rich, but in this case, if the courts declared him innocent of wrongdoing with Lord Gillion's gold against him, then he must have been openly innocent. So much so that the courts had no choice but to let him go."

A man in the back said, "It was a smart thing to put that poster up. Many thought he had turned bad. Now we know the truth. He will be welcome in my home and without fear of my telling."

Nearly everyone agreed with the man. I said to myself, "Good, that will slow down the assassins."

Riders were coming up, so I backed off into the woods a little. It took a few more seconds for the others to realize that horses were coming. I recognized the lead rider, Lord Fantail, baron of this valley.

Baron Fantail dismounted, and the people bowed and parted. He looked at the new poster and read it closely. Aloud he said, "So that is what Lord Gillion is up to these days. Doesn't like my court's decisions and takes matters into his own hands, does he? It seems that our hero knight is declaring war against the barons and dukes if they help him in any way." He laughed long and hard. "You have to love a good fighter." He stood in thought for a minute and then called his second in charge over. "Dorn, have all affiliations with Lord Gillion cut. We do not buy from him, we do not use his ships, we do not allow him to visit, and we do not visit him. Ensure he does not sell to us through middlemen. I want nothing to do with the fool. Do not allow his ships in my harbor or his caravans on my roads, and give him thirty days to remove all his belongings from my city. That includes his warehouses. In thirty days we confiscate everything he has not moved, especially his lands."

The second bowed, and with a wicked grin he said, "As you wish, my lord baron. It shall be done."

The baron said, "Always wanted an excuse to take his warehouses. They will make fine barracks for my men and right on the docks. Great location." He turned and left to the applause of the people. He stopped and looked at them thoughtfully and said to his second, "Do it with prejudice. I don't want him thinking we want him back if he lives through this war." He turned and left.

I stood there wondering how many others would use this as an excuse to confiscate his empire. Interesting twist. I had not thought of this. I was ready to do some investigating. I knew I might have to change my plan, as I was previously going to burn down his warehouses. No sense upsetting the barons if I didn't need to.

Eight weeks later, I had gathered thousands of bits of information about Lord Gillion, and his empire was crashing down around his neck. Nearly half the ports in three countries were closed to his ships. My friends and many of the people I adventured with came to help me with this war. I had eighteen wizards, seven clerics, twenty-one rogues, and eighty-nine fighters under my command. They were not mercenaries; they were friends. And they were willing to take this to the lord and his friends and finish this war for me. However, I had better plans.

Two weeks later we rode into the city of Darvy, one of the few ports still friendly to Lord Gillion. We were met by the local baron's troops, and they were not happy that we outnumbered them and our people were more experienced and better provisioned. That plunder I talked about was paying the way and making us rich.

I rode to the front, asking, "Who is in charge?"

A seasoned captain said, "That would be me. Baron Kaylor does not want your army inside his borders."

I leaned forward in my saddle, and my troops took the sign and moved into an aggressive position instantly. Wizards were flying, and arrows were nocked. The captain started sweating. "I have word and proof that your baron is helping Lord Gillion. Tomorrow you will need a new baron. He has forfeited his life. I will give you this day to remove his wife and children. Do not take the baron with you. You will be watched."

He tried to say something, but we rode right past him as if he were nothing. He and his men rode hard to reach the baron's estates before we could. They removed the wife and children and all the servants. We passed them on the way. The wife motioned for us to stop.

I did. "How may I help you, baroness?"

"Why is it you are letting us go free?"

"It is my understanding that you stood against your husband's foolish loyalties to Lord Gillion. I also know that you and the baron are not, shall we say, compatible. He seems to like other or additional women."

Heat coursed through her face, and there was loathing behind her eyes—and it wasn't for me. She answered, "It is common knowledge. It is also common knowledge that you sacked and completely destroyed the last two port towns that helped Lord Gillion."

I said, "Before your marriage, you ran this city and the valley very well and your people prospered. Your appointed husband took over, as is the law, and everything has gone downhill since then. I would simply have you back on the seat of power. You do not have to go far. Tomorrow you will still have a city. I am not going to destroy it at this time. I am simply here to remove Lord Gillion's pet and put you in his place. I will wait thirty days to see what you do before revisiting your city in my plans."

She smiled. "I will follow, and this time when my husband expires, I will mourn his loss for ten years. Therefore, the king cannot appoint me another."

I allowed her to have the last word, as I happened to know she liked it that way. We rode past her and directly to the estates. One of my rogues came to me and said, "He is inside, sir, with a messenger from Lord Gillion."

I dismounted and drew my sword. Others started to come with me, but I said, "Mine!" and they backed off. I walked up to the door and knocked. No one answered. I kicked the heavy oak door in, and it splintered as it slammed against the stone wall. "Baron!"

A fat little man with another man, taller and more assured, stepped out. The baron had a heavy crossbow in his hand, and it was pointed at me. He fired, and I raised my blade, deflecting the crossbow bolt—a little trick I picked up from the elves. Two steps and the messenger was dead. I killed him first, as I knew from descriptions that it was Lord Gillion's sorcerer. One should always kill the magic user first to avoid being turned into something unnatural. The baron begged for his life and swore he would do everything in his power to help in my war against Lord Gillion.

A shadow fell into the room, so I was on guard. A voice behind me at the door said, "Sir Knight, are you going to believe my lying husband's words?"

I cut his head off, and as it rolled across the floor, I said, "Not likely."

As I walked out, I said in passing, "Do not disappoint me, baroness."

She said, "You did me a big favor, so I will do you one. Lord Gillion is sending twenty ships to Hanty to take that island port."

I said, "Hanty is not friendly with Gillion."

She said, "*Take* is not a friendly word."

"When?"

"First spring."

"Thank you."

I walked out, and before leaving, I heard the baroness yell orders to have the bodies burned without burial or ceremony. Then she said,

"Lord Gillion is rat meat, Captain. You know what we do with rats in this city."

"I'm on it, my lady. It is nice to see you back in charge."

My lead wizard sent word to Hanty. The word back was that they were wide open and could do nothing about it. Orders came to withdraw all troops from the islands.

I sat at the camp thinking. *To remove all the protections that the king has built up over the years from the isles would take power. The power of a duke.* I had my wizard send word to a good friend of mine that worked for the king, the royal wizard, Lazar.

"Lazar, someone has removed all the protections from the isles, and now I find that Lord Gillion is going to take over Hanty by force and make it his fort hideaway."

The word instantly came back. "I will tell the king and get word back as quickly as possible, my friend."

Within an hour, the word came back. "The king was most upset. The admiral is turning around and will be waiting for Lord Gillion's ships. The admiral's words were, 'We could use some good ships for the fleet, and Lord Gillion just forfeited them.' The king orders you to find Duke Tomas and remove him from power. The orders to remove the troops from the islands came from him."

We pulled up camp and headed out toward the City of Eight Rivers, where Duke Tomas resided. We did not ride straight into the city or the lands, because the duke had an army of hundreds. The rogues brought back information that the duke was in his palace. I sent word to the duke that I was going to destroy his city for allowing Lord Gillion to use it freely. I gave him warning that the destruction would start in one week. The Duke immediately sent all his men to warn the city, set up for defense, and protect his holdings. Thinking himself safe for one week, he stayed behind to pack with a small contingent of fifty armed men, one wizard, and one cleric. We hit him unaware that night. He put up a good battle, but they had no chance. I faced him in the courtyard. His men were dead, his family was in the city, and his servants had fled. He was alone. He drew sword and dirk and faced me like a man. He did not last long, and he did not beg. He knew he was caught when I told him it was on the king's orders.

"Found out, did he. I wasn't expecting the king to find out so quickly. In a couple of days, I would have had everything covered up. Shame he found out so soon. I take it you're not here to destroy the city?"

"No, the king's coming down with an army to place someone loyal to him on the ducal throne."

"Well, my subjects are loyal to the king even if I was not. They will not fight His Majesty. You let him know that this was all my doing. No one else was a party to my decision."

"Except, of course, Lord Gillion."

"Of course. I suppose you think me a traitor?"

It was at that time I feinted. He moved in too quickly for the advantage, and my blade shot up under his breastplate and into his heart. "It matters not what I think."

I walked away amid shouts of victory from my men.

Gillion's ships attacked Hanty as planned, and they were taken by the king. Gillion's riches lay in waste, his power was gone, and his protections were running.

An assassin came to me and said, "Lord Gillion can no longer afford the price for your head, Sir Knight. I am here to let you know we will not be attacking you any—"

I killed him before he could finish his words. I don't like assassins.

We were joined by two thousand of the king's best men on the day we marched into Gillion's port town. It was reported that he was there and in his palace. I went in with my men, and he was hanging from a beam. He was ruined, and all that he had worked for had been destroyed or was in the hands of his competitors. He had taken his own life. I was sorely disappointed.

Rogues researched, and we knew their positions. We marched to the Assassin's Guild. We blocked every entrance—and we knew them all, including the secret passageways—and set fire to their headquarters. At the same time, the king's men and my men were hitting eight other headquarters in eight major cities. Hundreds died in the contained fires.

It would be a long time before they returned, but maybe, just maybe, they would remember that some contracts might not be worth the gold.

# The Assassin

The contract wasn't supposed to be difficult. There weren't supposed to be guards, war dogs, and tiny dragons protecting the lady. I watched the little forest manor house from the tree I had been sitting in for the last three hours. They had two wizards using Correct Vision spells. I could see their eyes aglow with magic. They had an eye sundry. Where did they get an elder eye sundry?! There is nothing better for keeping watch than an eye sundry. They can see in the dark, and often, they can see invisible objects. The eyes on their twenty stalks can look in all directions, and each stalk has a ray of light it can use to light up the enemy. Very costly. I could also see the ghostly outlines of a wraith and several undead specters.

This subject had been warned, but by whom? It wasn't one of the brotherhood. No, the penalty for betrayal was far too brutal for anyone to go astray. Once part of the brotherhood, always part of the brotherhood, unless—no, that could not be. Someone of higher ranking wants me dead. He or she could order someone to warn the target or someone close to her and then just sit back and wait. That would explain the timeline. She probably could not afford to keep up this kind of protection for long, if at all.

Another possibility was that she might be protected by one of the brotherhood. It was possible that another had taken a protection contract unknowingly. That had happened before, and it was always messy. Having a protection contract on someone you have a hit contract on—not good. I slowly climbed down from my vantage point and made a wide circle around the home while looking for another of the brotherhood. If a protection contract was in place, then the brotherhood would be present. If it was a hit contract on me, then the brotherhood would not be present. I watched the eye sundry's eye stalks. At one point, one stalk turned quickly to the roof.

There, on the roof, by the third stovepipe, was a bump in the tiles. I watched the bump for about thirty minutes before it moved just the tiniest bit. There would not be two of the brotherhood. That would cost far more than this lady could possibly afford, and backers would shy away at the cost of two.

So someone in the brotherhood wanted her alive, and someone wanted her dead. Not my problem. I held the contract for her death, and either she would be dead or I would be, and I didn't intend for it to be me.

I let fly with a blow dart at the bump on the roof. A second later it silently collapsed. The eye sundry noticed the movement, but there wasn't enough for alarm. I worked my way toward the roof ever so slowly. Several times the war-dogs started barking, but never at me; once they barked at a skunk, and once a fox. The miniature dragons always went to investigate, but the eye sundry stayed put. Dragons have blind sense, even tiny ones, and if any animals had caused the dogs to bark in my direction, I would have been in for it. You can't hide from blind sense. Also, the wraith could sense my spirit. If it came close, it would know immediately.

I left the tree. Taking my time so I wouldn't be noticed, I made it to the side of the house in only five hours. I was on the opposite side of the structure from the eye sundry. I waited for the guards to part on their perimeter walk. When they did, I climbed up the side of the house and onto the roof. An hour later I made it to the brother. He was dead from my poison dart. I took the dart and placed it in my pouch. I pulled the boy away from the tarp he had been using to blend into the roof, while keeping the tarp up enough to look occupied to the eye sundry. Then I stuffed the boy into the chimney on the far side of the house. They were not likely to use it at that time of year. Not in that heat.

I climbed under the tarp and looked out from the tiny holes tactically placed around the edges. I moved down toward the side with the eye sundry while keeping the tarp over my body. The eye sundry noticed immediately but said nothing. The guards and the war dogs did nothing. The undead stayed in place. I left the tarp and, in front of everyone, I climbed down the wall. I blended in well, but as expected, a few saw me. The eye sundry said something to a guard captain, and he walked over.

The captain asked in a whisper, "Why are you not on the roof as you told everyone you should be?"

I said, "I have seen nothing, and for the other to show this quickly would be near impossible. It will take him another two days at best."

"Not if he used magic. You know the bet has a timeline."

"We do not rely on others, especially magic users. Besides, I need to use the privy."

He said to me, "It's inside and down the hall in the back of the house. Be quick."

I walked inside and down the hall. As I passed a little room, I saw the lady sitting in a chair surrounded by several guards. Something was wrong. She was slouching. Grand Ladies don't slouch. Even when crying, their backs are as stiff and as straight as a masterwork arrow, mostly because of their corsets.

I found the privy, and it was locked. I gently knocked.

A woman's voice said, "Who dares!"

It was a very commanding voice. A high-born lady's voice. There was a touch of fear in that voice. A servant would be far more afraid. I answered, "It is the dark one, lady."

"Did something go wrong? Am I in danger?"

I smiled for the first time in three days. This was the lady of my contract. Note that she did not ask about the servant decoy. What lady would care about a servant?"

"When you are done, my lady. I need to use the same."

"Drank too much wine at dinner, fool. They sent me an idiot. I will have words with Lord Foxmore."

Ah, Lord Foxmore. My contract had been given me by his childhood enemy. Politics made no difference to me; I had a contract, and that was all I needed. I placed my gloved finger into a small vial, pulled it out, and capped the vial. Then I waited.

The door unlocked and she came out dressed as a serving wench. I touched her arm, saying, "I am sorry, my lady." I went in looking like I was trying to hold it in and about to mess myself. That way I did not have to look her in the eye. The brotherhood kept their identities secret by keeping wrapped up completely. The brother on the roof had been dressed the exact same way I was.

She said, "You should be."

I finished my business in the privy, which included cleaning my glove. I then returned to the rooftop. From there I followed my path back down to the yard and out into the trees. I waited in my vantage point. Soon things started stirring about, and then anger erupted from the house. A man came out yelling to all the guards, "The lady is sick. Something is wrong. Get the assassin down here. Now!"

I watched as the lady-dressed serving girl tried to help the real lady. The cleric tried to counteract the poison, but it was not that kind. I had used a very expensive supernatural poison. He tried a full heal, but that did not help either. She died in the captain's arms. All through the night, I watched as people died. A smear of very slow poison on the privy seat ensured that the lady was dead, and the servant girl, and pretty much every human in the household. Before they died, they did mount a search in case I was still there. They found the dead brother. Shame having to do that, but he was the only real threat.

# The Cleric: The Wrong Questions

It was a bright, cheery morning; the songbirds were in grand form, and flowers were blooming in a profusion that nearly raped the senses with shades of every color imaginable. Smells changed with every step I took through the garden, and I did not care.

I walked quickly through the garden and into my sanctuary. I needed to meditate on the thoughts that were in multitude at the breakfast table. I had no argument to defend my church. Everything I said was logically shot down by the cleric of Valoris, and I needed to be prepared for lunch in case this topic continued, as I was sure it would.

I will never forget the beginning of the topic, which took place right in front of the princess.

"Your god that you speak of is not much of a lover of children, is he, friend cleric of Sobelli?"

"What do you mean, friend cleric of Valoris?"

"I never see your ilk down at the orphanage. None of your priests visit there. They had a sickness spread throughout their ranks, and your fellow worshippers did nothing, even though they were asked—in fact, begged."

"We were busy in the other districts trying to help out our own worshippers. The plague was rampant throughout the city, good cleric of Valoris."

"So true, my friend of Sobelli. However, did not the plague start at the orphanage, and if you had helped when asked, would your god not have given you the ability to stop the plague at that point so that it would not spread?"

I remember just staring at him until the princess asked, "Is this true, cleric of Sobelli?"

I answered, "When looking at the past, it is always easy to see what should have been done, what should have been the choice, my princess. When looking to the future and present, it is far more difficult."

The cleric of Valoris said, "True, so very true, friend of Sobelli. However, a little prayer told all the other clerics—the few there were—that the orphanage was to be cleansed."

In defense I said, "We used our abilities to protect our own from the possibility of catching the plague. We saved many lives. None that we protected caught the disease."

The cleric of Valoris said, "Very correct; all of those rich people that paid very handsomely lived without fear of the plague. The palace paid how much for the services of the clerics of Sobelli, Princess?"

She motioned a servant to her, and he whispered an amount and her eyes widened. "Tens of thousands of gold went to ensure all within the palace were kept clean of the plague, good cleric of Valoris."

"The fact is, Princess, the same clerics that you tend to shun because we do not care for grandeur and immense temples—Valoris, Potentis, Natura, even Proba of the elves—spent all their time in the poor quarters helping the poor and the middle class for free, and the clerics of Sobelli helped only the ones that could pay, and pay a lot. They made a considerable amount of money and have more worshipers of higher rank now that the plague is over than they ever had before. The Church of Sobelli increased greatly while the others spent everything they had to save lives."

The princess turned to me. "Is this true, cleric of Sobelli? Did even one of your clerics help the poor?"

"We were all busy helping our members, Princess. We have a lot, you know."

The cleric of Valoris said, "Yes, and many of them were poor and middle class. Yet, you did nothing for them."

The princess asked, "Cleric of Sobelli, did you help your own people who could not afford to pay?"

I said, "I do not think we did. Orders from on high were to help our greatest benefactors first."

The cleric of Valoris dropped the rock on my foot then. "It seems interesting to me that the plague has spread only to the cities with wealth. No matter how well we stop the plague, it continues to show up every few years. In each case, the good clerics of Sobelli are there in force and only help the rich. Is it not true, good cleric of Sobelli, that you had more brothers than normal in your temple at the time of the breakout of plague this year and three years ago?"

Everyone knew that we did. "Good cleric of Valoris, you know it is true. What are you trying to insinuate?"

The cleric of Valoris sat back. "Only that it seems strange that you are always prepared with more brothers than usual, that you have more potions prepared than normal, and that you only cater to the wealthy and are the only church to profit from the plague. The rest of us suffer along with the other masses."

The princess stood and stormed out, saying, "I need to talk to Father."

I made it to my sanctuary and told the acolyte that I did not wish to be disturbed, as I was going to commune with our god. The acolyte's eyes nearly popped out when he heard I was going to break the dictum to never bypass the higher church members and go directly to God without their permission. He left after stationing two brothers at my door.

I went to knee and started the spell. Communing with God is difficult and costly, and it allows one to receive only yes or no answers. Sometimes those answers are vague. I asked the following and was surprised by the answers:

"My great and wonderful God, is the Church of Sobelli responsible for the plague spreading?"

"*Yes.*"

That was an unexpected answer and caused all my other questions to be useless. *Think, think, boy. Ask the right questions. You can only do this once.*

"My great and wonderful God, is the current leader of the Church, the pope, knowledgeable of this blasphemy?"

"*Yes.*"

Another unexpected answer. *Now, what would drive the pope to do something he should not do?*

"My great and wonderful God, is the rest of the council aware of what the pope is doing?"

"*Yes.*"

*The rest of the council knows?! For all that is good in the world,* why? "My great and wonderful God, is the pope doing this of his own accord?"

"*No.*"

*Okay, if he is not doing this of his own accord, then someone is pulling his puppet strings. Who?*

"My great and wonderful God, is someone controlling my pope against his will?"

"Sort of."

*Vague, but this points to someone else making us do this. Who would stand to gain from causing all these deaths?*

"My great and wonderful God, is it someone within the Church of Sobelli?"

"*No.*"

*Ah, someone outside the Church is pulling the strings.*

"My great and wonderful God, can you strike down this foe?"

"*Yes* and *no.*"

*Interesting answer—he can, but something must be holding him back. What could hold back my god? No other god is powerful enough.*

"My great and wonderful God, could you strike them down if there were no balance issues?"

"Yes."

*Ah, the balance between good and evil would become unbalanced and therefore allow evil into our world unchecked. That must mean that a good-aligned god unbalanced the scale and allowed evil in, and so a rebalance happened, or evil found a way to control my pope without the need to enter into this world.*

"My great and wonderful God, can you lead me to the one doing this?"

"*Yes.*"

*Ah, then it is one, and probably a champion of some sort of evil god.*

"My great and wonderful God, can I defeat this blasphemer?"

"*Yes* and *no.*"

*Interesting—it can be defeated, but I cannot.*

"My great and wonderful God, can I defeat him with help from other brothers?"

"*No.*"

*Another perplexing issue. Our brothers cannot defeat the creature, but someone else can.*

"My great and wonderful God, can I defeat him with the help of the Church of Valoris?"

"*Yes.*"

*That is the clue I needed. Our brothers would be ordered to stop and would listen. The brothers of the Church of Valoris are not consigned to take orders from our pope. That means two things. First, I need their*

*help, and second, the wrongdoer is within the highest level of the Church,*
*where it can directly control my pope.*

"My great and wonderful God, is this intruder hiding within
the highest level of the Church, where it can directly control my
pope?"

"*Yes.*"

The contact was ended, and I collapsed to the floor. When I
awoke, I was instantly surrounded by my brothers. One asked, "You
contacted Sobelli?"

"I did, and you would not believe what I found out."

"Kill him."

They beat me to death using their morningstars. As I entered my
god's presence, I was instantly aware that I was dead.

A solar stood at the gate to the Caelum temple and asked,
"Father, do you wish to venture what you did wrong that got you
killed?"

I thought for only a second. "I underestimated how far this evil
has spread?"

"No, you did not ask the one question you needed to ask."

"And what did I need to ask, great seraphim?"

"Is this your will, oh God?"

# The Gladiator

I stood at guard waiting in the center of the largest royal arena in the country. The tall spires of the castle and the large statues of the gods did not distract me from my current battle. There is a moment before the battle where everything seems to slow down, where each moment lasts a lifetime, where time stops. I was in that moment and doing what makes me better than the others. I was using that time to find weakness in my challengers.

One of the fools was wearing full plate of golden hue. Magical, no doubt. At this level nearly all the combatants, except me, wear magical everything and have magical weapons. He had no shield, as he was sporting a grand two-handed great sword. The blade glowed and shimmered in the noonday sun. I was sure he knew how to use it against someone as big as I, but he did not study me very well. If he had, he would have known that magically bypass metals on his sword would not work against me. I wear no armor. And if he did not study me, he did not know my options. That was his weakness.

The second wore only light armor. His two rapiers were twin blades of magic, and he was showing off just how quick he could be. His blades were a blur. His pathetic attempt to put a little fright in me was useless. I do not frighten so easily. He tried to hide in plain sight. Nice trick, and it marked him as a rogue. He did not study me either, or he would have known I had "Sense Living" as a supernatural ability. Another group of fools. Last year about this time I fought a single opponent, and he nearly defeated me. He studied my fights. He knew me, and I could tell. The weapons he brought did the greatest possible damage, his armor gave him the most possible advantage, and his tactics changed with mine. I actually had to think to defeat him. I let him live, as I like a good challenge. However, these two were not going to be much of a challenge, and that would disappoint the crowd. Their tactic was easy to see. The full-plate fighter was going to keep me busy while the rogue sneak attacked me in the back. Good tactic to use twenty years ago. I am better than that now.

The prince stood and raised a hand. Time sped up to its normal pace. He lowered his hand, and they started to circle in opposite directions—a common ploy to allow them to reach either side of me for flanking. I went invisible. It is hard to flank and sneak attack when you cannot see where the enemy's vital organs are.

They looked frightened. I suppose they were thinking that their requirement for this to be a tournament to the death was possibly not a good idea. I stayed put to see what they would do.

The foolish fighter was nothing to me, but he could move fairly quickly and had lots life in him. While sporting that sword, he would take some time to kill; however, if he panicked, I could finish this fairly quickly. The rogue was not so full of life. He was small and fast but would die very quickly. I decided to kill the rogue first and then play with the fighter for a short time. It's always good to be outside for a while, and I decided that as soon as I destroyed these two, and after lunch, I was going to take a long, restful walk in the forest.

I waited, thinking, *Let them come to me. They will search when they realize that I am not going to come out of hiding.* The prince stood up and motioned to my second. I knew he wanted to see something happen. He is so impatient. I took one step and picked up the tiny rogue. The crowd, consisting of all the royal family, the generals and captains of the army, and the admirals and top mates of the navy, went wild. I tossed him at the stands right in front of the prince. The magical shield held, as it always does, but it allowed the blood to stay on the shield and smear down as the rogue fell thirty feet to the ground. Then there was a tiny ripple in the shield and the blood was gone.

The rogue lay there as the fighter yelled, "Get up! For God's sake, Eleanor, get up!"

He headed toward his friend, which was a mistake. I backhanded the fool, and he landed some eighty feet away on the other side of the arena. His armor was bent and broken in places, and he had to remove his helm to see. I was in shock. It was a half-elf. I had to think back to remember how long it had been since I fought and killed a half-elf. *Oh well, he volunteered for this fight, and so he shall have it.*

I walked over to the rogue knowing full well his life force was doing well. He was faking being unconscious. It was easy to tell even without my magic. He had not dropped his swords; both were still in his hands. An unconscious elf or human would have let go of the swords. It's just natural. I picked him up again and tossed him to the other side of the arena, right into his friend, bowling them both over. The crowd always liked that move, and they cheered me on. Humans are so bloodthirsty.

I silently moved around the arena to just behind them. One pulled out a potion and started to drink it. I slapped it out of his hand. The potion broke on the ground. The fighter took that moment to attack where I was standing. His blade bounced off my hide. It stung a little. I roared just to let the crowd know he had hit me. The crowd was in shock and stood up, wondering if this would be the day.

Thirty-six years I have reigned as champion of the ring. Thirty-six years of killing for the pleasure of humans. I was sick of it and started having thoughts about letting these two kill me. I looked at them and decided, *Nope! Not these fools. If I'm going to allow someone to kill me, it needs to be someone with a little talent. These two have none.*

I said to the crowd and the team, "Foolish half-elves. Did you not think to bring anything to make me visible? Maybe a potion of Seeing Invisible or some glitter dust? Or did I just destroy your only potion?"

They both attacked where my voice came from, but being twenty feet tall gives me the chance to lean over and talk. They did not know where I truly was, as my voice was directly over their heads and they couldn't jump that high.

The fighter yelled, "Show yourself. Give us that much of a chance."

The crowd cheered and started chanting, "Show yourself! Show yourself!"

Loud enough for the entire crowd to hear over their chanting, I said, "So be it." I took five steps away from them and became visible. My back was against the wall, and my right side was against one of the columns. They could not flank me. They stood away from my reach, trying to get me to leave my position.

"Come on, monster. Fight us. Come over here and attack us again." They called me names, and I ignored them for a while until one said, "You can't end this battle from there."

I smiled and said for everyone to hear, "I can wait until you starve to death. I can last a lot longer than you."

The crowd did not like that. They wanted blood. Oh well. The rogue and fighter turned around to motion for the crowd to pressure me. As they turned back, I jumped to the other side of the two, grabbed the rogue, and ran to the other side of the arena. I started beating him against the wall. By the time the fighter reached me, I had killed the rogue twice over. Blood was everywhere, and the crowd was going wild.

Now that it was only the fighter, I walked to the center of the ring, saying, "Come, little half-elf. I am waiting. Your death will be very slow, as I have plenty of time before lunch."

He charged, and as I let him through my space, he took a mighty backswing and actually cut me just a little as he passed by. His smile turned to fear as he watched me quickly heal myself. I heard him say, "Fast healing."

I reached out and grabbed his sword. "Did you not study my other fights? Everyone knows I have fast healing, they know I can turn invisible, and they know I am magical." I used his sword to pick out an arm bone from my back molars. I smiled and handed him back his sword, saying, "Pardon, but breakfast was stuck in my teeth."

He dropped his sword and ran toward the gate, but this fight was to the death. I walked up to him and picked him up and then walked over to the king and prince and asked, "Why, foolish half-elf? Why did you decide to fight me to the death? It is sad to have to destroy you in front of all these people, but you left me no choice."

He said, "It was the gold. The price for killing you in the arena is great. Enough to set us up for life."

I smiled as I pulled off his right arm. "Life is very short. Filling it with gold is a waste." As I pulled off a leg I continued, "You should have realized that life is far more precious than gold. You should fill it with love, learning, and hard work." I pulled off his head and dropped him on the ground.

I turned to the king and asked, "Majesty, what's for lunch? Half-elf is too stringy."

The crowd went wild.

# The Illusionist

"Hello."

The fighter looked all around for the voice, as did the others. Again I said, "Hello, why are you trying to open my door? I did not hear a knock."

The one dressed like a cleric asked, "Who are you?"

"Interesting. You try to break into my mountain home, and you do not even know who lives here? I am Gordomerious. Most call me Gord. Who are you? And please tell that one dressed in black to stop trying to unlock my door and put the trap back in place. Thank you."

"Gord, we are adventurers and did not know that anyone lived in these ruins. They have been vacant for a long time."

The apparent rogue was still trying to unlock my door. I said, "It seems you have been misinformed. I have been living in this house for millennia, and it is not ruins. Did you not notice how well groomed the walkway is? The path through the forest was easy to follow and well taken care of, was it not? This home is in great condition. The walls are all intact, the mortar fresh, and the doors all hung properly. Your friend is still trying to open my door. Please have him stop."

"Gord, what are you?"

The rogue finished unlocking my door.

"Who I am or what I am is not important. Who you are is, since you have now broken into my home and are considered thieves and possibly assassins." I closed the door in their face and relocked it. Then I put the trap back in place with a little extra surprise in case they tried to bash the door down.

The fighter said, "Show yourself, Gord, or whatever you are. Prove you are not a ghost or something haunting this ruin."

"Haunting! A ghost! Since when does a specter of any kind take care of the surroundings? When have you ever seen a ghost that mortared the walls?"

The fighter smiled. "I will admit this is a first."

The cleric said, "We have been told that there are creatures of the night up here. Creatures that are unnatural."

"The only unnatural creatures in these parts are the humans that live in the village below and the two humans in your party of thieves, dwarf. Did the village send you?"

"They warned us away, Gord. It is the king that sent us."

"Well, the villagers are more intelligent than the king. I think I have been very nice to them. I allowed them to set up a small town on my land. I have not eaten any of them. Several times over the last forty years, I have protected them from others. I think I deserve respect and to be left alone."

*Boom!* The rogue was quick and did not take any damage from my fireball trap, but the others were not so lucky. I laughed.

The fighter angrily asked, "What's so funny?"

"Your beard is smoking."

He looked down and quickly put it out. "That was not nice, Gord."

"I told you to leave the door alone, and you knew it was trapped. You brought that upon yourself."

The rogue said, "Stand back a little farther, please. Forty feet should be enough."

I quickly reset the trap with an additional element to the fireball.

They watched as the rogue tried again. The fireball went off, and the rogue evaded it again; the others, again, did not. They had moved outside of the normal fireball's spread, but I had added an element that widened it. The fireball had taken up twice the space as normal. I laughed.

The fighter was even angrier. "*Not funny!*"

"Your beard is on fire."

The dwarf looked down and beat the fire out with his hand. Half his beard was gone. I laughed some more and said, "Keep this up and we will have a bald dwarf."

The cleric chuckled as he healed them.

I had noticed how the party lined up, so I changed the trap and reset it.

The wizard and cleric were doing spells to resist my fire trap, so the new trap that I placed used electricity. The rogue accidently tripped the trap, and a ball of lighting slammed down the steps and into the group. Everyone got caught, including the rogue. I laughed and said, "You need a better rogue."

The fighter said, "We need new tactics. The front door does not work."

I said, "The front door works fine. You could try knocking and asking politely." They all looked at the door, thinking, but they decided against it and started looking for another entrance.

It took two days for them to find the back door. I said, "It's about time you found the rear entrance. I was getting bored waiting for you to set off these traps."

The rogue was about to try the door but backed away after hearing my statement. I teased, "Chicken! "Bawk bok bok bok, *bawwwwwk* bok bok bok bok."

The fighter said, "I'm glad you have a sense of humor. You will need it when I get my hands on you."

"I must warn you, dwarf, that if you enter my home without permission, you will become food."

"I am told that I am tough and stringy, Gord."

"The last dwarf that illegally entered my home was very tasty, and his armor crunchy. The beard was a little difficult to choke down. Live and learn; I'll burn yours off before eating you. May I make a suggestion?"

The cleric said, "Go ahead."

"Go back to the king and tell him that he is no longer welcome on my land and that I said that if he continues to send creatures to attack me, I will remove him. So far, I have left the humans alone. However, if this foolishness continues, it will change things."

The fighter said, "We do not plan on leaving you alive to attack the king. I hear you have gold up here."

"Ah, there it is. You are here for stealing, and you would kill me to get what I may or may not have. Did the villagers tell you I was wealthy? I do not see how they would know, as they have never visited."

The wizard asked, "They said nothing. It was others that told us. The villagers have never entered your home?"

"I invited them when they first started to settle here, but they did not come. I was most disappointed."

The wizard said, "You do know that the king believes he owns this land."

"He probably does. Humans are so possessive. However, his kind has only been here for a couple thousand years. I have been here before the mountains were created. Irritating, that." I could see the disbelief in the dwarf's eyes.

The wizard asked, "Irritating that the king believes he owns the land?"

"No, little human. It is irritating that I continuously have to rebuild my home every few thousand years. This home started out in a nice valley created by glaciers. The two mountain ranges have pushed against each other and caused one large mountain range to form. Another glacier came and cut the valley you see below us. I have rebuilt this home hundreds of times."

The dwarf stood in silence until he finally said, "You cannot have lived that long. Even the stupid elves don't live that long."

I laughed and laughed.

The fighter asked, "What is so funny, Gord?"

"Your inability to understand, dwarf. You are entering my temple. I have been here since before the first elf. Before most of the gods you know. I will always be here. This is my home, and you are intruders."

The cleric asked, "If you are so powerful, then why don't you simply destroy us?"

"How about I destroy the village instead."

A loud explosion came from below, and the village was gone—wiped off the face of the earth. "The next thing I will destroy is the capital city. You have five minutes to leave."

They scrambled down the mountain to their horses and road at breakneck speed through the empty, burnt-out place where the village used to be. They rode until their horses were near exhaustion. Magically, I watched them each day, and on the second day, they teleported to the capital city and spoke with the king.

"Majesty, we have failed in our mission."

"You are still alive. How could you fail and all still be intact?"

The fighter said, "You did not tell us it was an ancient god we were fighting, Sire. He destroyed an entire village with just one word. He said that if we did not leave, the capital city would be next. We could not take the chance that he was telling the truth."

The wizard said, "Even if he was not telling the truth, he is evidently far more powerful than we thought. He showed godlike powers. We are no match for that kind of ability. Our rogue could not open his door or get past his traps. It is my opinion that we should leave his temple alone and forbid others from pestering him."

"Then you believe he is harmless if left alone?"

"Yes, Majesty. He told us that all he wanted was some respect and to be left alone."

The king sat in thought. It took a little time, but he finally said, "Very well. I hope you are correct in this. We will leave him alone and build our road around his temple. Way around his temple. That valley and the mountain are now off-limits, and I will station a garrison at the pass to ensure it."

I stopped scrying on the fighter after hearing the king's words. Everything worked wonderfully, including the fake village I had destroyed by simply dispelling the magic and placing a burnt illusion in its place; the fake door they could never get through, which allowed me to cast spells from the real entrance; the outside looking like it was just repaired; and talking directly into their heads in a benevolent but strong voice. All of it made those fools think this was an old god's temple.

Now I can examine all the treasure I've found in this ancient ruin at my leisure. Thousands of books, enough gold to swim in, jewels, priceless art, and artifacts by the dozen—all mine for the taking. All the denizens had fled or died from the illusions I created to chase them out.

I am rich beyond my wildest dreams, and all because I chose a path the others in my class shunned. My peers and the wizards at the university said I'd never make it as an illusionist. That I should go into something more substantial. Well, the illusion is on them.

**The End**

# About the Author

John Ricks was born in Longview, Washington, and moved thirteen times before he finished middle school. After graduating high school, he joined the navy, where he spent twenty more years traveling the world, meeting new and astonishing people. His degrees, extensive reading, and travel have given him ample fuel for fantasy and science fiction dreams. He has developed a great sense of fantasy and a powerful love for writing.